D0980103

I WENT TO THE WINDOW.

Yep, you could see for miles.

And do you know what you could see for miles? Sheep. Oh no, there are some pigs.

I put my bag down on the bed. My bed, by the way, is wooden. It's got wood carvings all over it. Even the bed-head has got furry things carved into it. Squirrels, I think. Or maybe hairy, long-tailed slugs.

I put my secret letter from Georgia under my pillow. For luck.

I unpacked my suitcase and hung my clothes up in the (wooden) wardrobe. I must start planning what to wear for my first day at Dother Hall. I wonder if we are allowed makeup? At my school, if we had worn makeup we would have had our heads cut off. And put on the school gates as a warning to others.

But hahahahaha, I am on my own now.

I am flying solo.

Also by Louise Rennison

The (Mis)Adventures of Tallulah Casey series:

A MIDSUMMER TIGHTS DREAM

The Confessions of Georgia Nicolson books:

ANGUS, THONGS AND FULL-FRONTAL SNOGGING

ON THE BRIGHT SIDE, I'M NOW THE
GIRLFRIEND OF A SEX GOD

KNOCKED OUT BY MY NUNGA-NUNGAS

DANCING IN MY NUDDY-PANTS

AWAY LAUGHING ON A FAST CAMEL

THEN HE ATE MY BOY ENTRANCERS

STARTLED BY HIS FURRY SHORTS

LOVE IS A MANY TROUSERED THING

STOP IN THE NAME OF PANTS!

ARE THESE MY BASOOMAS I SEE BEFORE ME?

WiTHERING TiGHTS

Louise Rennison

HARPER TEEN
An Imprint of HarperCollinsPublishers

HarperTeen is an imprint of HarperCollins Publishers.

Withering Tights
Copyright © 2011 by Louise Rennison Ltd
All rights reserved. Printed in the United States of America.
No part of this book may be used or reproduced in any manner whatsoever without
written permission except in the case of brief quotations embodied in critical articles
and reviews. For information address HarperCollins Children's Books, a division of
HarperCollins Publishers, 10 East 53rd Street, New York, NY 10022.
www.epicreads.com

Library of Congress Cataloging-in-Publication Data
Rennison, Louise.
Withering tights / by Louise Rennison. — 1st ed.
    p. cm.
    Summary: Self-conscious about her knobby knees but confident in her acting ability,
fourteen-year-old Tallulah spends the summer at a Yorkshire performing arts camp
that, she is surprised to learn, is for girls only.
    ISBN 978-0-06-179933-4 (pbk.)
    [1. Interpersonal relations—Fiction. 2. Camps—Fiction. 3. Performing arts—Fiction.
4. Self-confidence—Fiction. 5. Yorkshire (England)—Fiction. 6. England—Fiction.
7. Humorous stories.] I. Title.
PZ7.R2905Wit 2011   2010045552
[Fic]—dc22   CIP
                                                                                 AC

Typography by Becky Terhune
12 13 14 15 16   CG/RRDH   10 9 8 7 6 5 4 3 2 1
❖
First paperback edition, 2012

To all the Yorkshire heroes and hero-esses, the Cock and family, Leeds United past and present, Mum, Dad, sister, all cousins and second cousins forty-times removed, nieces, grandparents, great-grandparents (with particular thanks for the hiddly diddly diddly), Big Fat Bobbins and the Wilsons (particularly Mae, Queen of the tripe stall), and Kaiser Chiefs. And of course to the inventors of Withering Tights, Em, Chazza, and Anne Brontë.

And especially for all of you who've never been to God's Own Country (Yorkshire), I want to say, I'm sorry. Sorry that you've never felt the thud of driving hail on your face in the summer or tasted pig trotters. This book is the next best thing. It is. This is for you.

And Tara, as my American editor, thank you for everything. I will reward you with your very own cow heel to chew when you come over. Something to look forward to as a vegetarian.

Contents

Wow. This is it. This is me growing up. On my own, going to Performing Arts College. This is good-bye, Tallulah, you long, gangly thing, and helloooooo, Lullah, star of stage and . . . owwwwooo. Ow and ow.

The train lurched and I've nearly knocked myself out on the side of the door. I'm bound to get a massive lump. Oh good, I can start college with two heads. . . .

I've been reading my brochure about the summer school. It has a picture of a big manor house and underneath it says:

Welcome to Dother Hall. This magnificent center of the performing and visual arts nestles among the beautiful Yorkshire Dales.

The staff and friendly local people offer a warm

hand of encouragement to all of our prospective students. Think Wuthering Heights *but with more acting and dancing and less freezing to death on the moors!!*

Well, it was either this or going on an Outward Bound course with my little brother, Connor. The last time I went camping with him he cooked a dead butterfly and made it into a sandwich for me. For a laugh. He put tomato sauce on it.

I've been looking over the top of my brochure at the bloke opposite. He is the grumpiest man in the universe probably.

He's got no hair on his head, but he has loads of red hair shooting out of his ears. Like there are a couple of red squirrels nesting in there. Which would be quite good, actually, as they are an endangered species.

His wife said to him, "Oooh look, Fred, the sun's coming out."

And he said, "It can please its bloody self."

Is this what Yorkshire folk are like?

I wonder if anyone is missing me at home?

It will be next week before my grandma notices that my eggcup hasn't been used. I tried to explain to her that I was going to performing arts college in Yorkshire for the summer, and she said, "Will you bring a trifle back?"

Maybe she thought I said I was going to Marks and Spencers for the summer.

Mum didn't comment because as usual she wasn't there. She's gone to Norway to paint.

Not people's houses. She's doing her art.

When I stayed over with Cousin Georgia last night, I asked her what sort of painting the Norwegians did and she said, "It's mostly sledges."

I thought she meant they painted sledges a lot, but she said, "No, my not-so-little cousy, they paint WITH sledges."

She said the official term for that kind of work was "Sled-werk," and that it was one of the reasons why Norwegians had such big arms and had therefore become Vikings (for the rowing). And that if I dropped "Sled-werk" into a conversation at art college, people would be impressed.

Georgia knows a lot of stuff. Not just about painting, but about life. And boys. She wears a bra. It's a big one. She showed me her special disco inferno dancing and her lady bumps were jiggling quite a lot.

I wish I wore a bra. And jiggled.

It's so boring being fourteen and a half.

She's nice to me, but I know she thinks I'm just a kid.

When I left she gave me her "special" comedy mustache. She's grown out of it and thought it would suit me. She said, "Always remember, Lullah, if in doubt, get your mustache out."

I do love Georgia and wish I lived near her. I haven't got a sister and it's not the same having a brother. Connor mostly likes to talk about what he's going to kick next.

And that I am like a daddy longlegs in a skirt.

And how he could win a kicking contest with a daddy longlegs.

Is that normal in a boy?

Well, all will be revealed when I start my new life at Dother Hall.

Georgia's also given me a secret note to read on my first day at college. She says she will write to me. But will she?

I feel a bit miz.

Usually in the holidays I stay with Grandma. It was she who filled in the Dother Hall form for me. In the section about "talents and special interests" she put "Irish dancing and ball games."

You would have thought that would be a definite "no" from them, but they accepted me. Perhaps they thought I was some kind of dancing juggler.

Anyway, it's only for five weeks and then there is an assessment and you get chosen to stay on or not in the proper school.

I will look at the college brochure again to get me in the creative zone.

Let me see.

Here is a photo of a girl leaping around in the dance studio. The caption says:

Eliza loses herself in the beauty of modern dance.

As far as dancewear is concerned Eliza has gone for big tights.

As indeed she needs to.

Oh, and here's a photo of a boy.

What on earth is he holding?

Let's see.

The caption says:

Martin has made an instrument. Here he is holding his own small lute.

Crumbs.

Martin has got very bright lips.

Perhaps he is a mouth-breather; that makes your lips go very red.

Or perhaps it is lipstick.

I suppose anything goes in the crazy world of dance and theater! Hey nonny no, this is my new world, the world of showbiz!

But what if the course is full of people who can sing and dance and everything, and are really confident?

And hate me because of my nobbly kneecaps?

★ ★ ★

Uh-oh, we are arriving at my station. I must get my bag down. I'll get up on the seat and try and reach it. . . . Oh great balls of fire, I've just accidentally kicked Mr. Squirrel as he was getting up.

What does, "You great big dunderwhelp, use your bloody gogglers!" mean in English?

I bet it's not nice.

His wife said, "Take no notice, love. If there was a moaning medal, he'd win it hands down."

I let them get off first.

How come everyone else in my family is the right height and I have knees that are four feet above the ground?

I swung the train door open and saw the sign:

Skipley
Home of the
West Riding Otter

There was a little bus to take us into Heckmondwhite. I didn't know sheep could go on buses, but they can. One was sitting next to me. Not on its own, I mean. It hadn't just got on with its bus pass. There was a woman in Wellingtons holding it.

She said to me, "I'd sit upwind if I were thee, love."

We bundled along on the bus on a road that went up and down dales. Along the skyline I could see the moorland the while . . . lalalalala," I looked around my new bijou home.

It's a sweet room really, you know, good, but I thought going to performing arts college might be more . . . gooderer.

I went to the window.

Yep, you could see for miles.

And do you know what you could see for miles? Sheep.

Oh no, there are some pigs.

I put my bag down on the bed. My bed, by the way, is wooden. It's got wood carvings all over it. Even the bed-head has got furry things carved into it. Squirrels, I think. Or maybe hairy, long-tailed slugs.

I put my secret letter from Georgia under my pillow. For luck.

I unpacked my suitcase and hung my clothes up in the (wooden) wardrobe. I must start planning what to wear for my first day at Dother Hall. It will be weird not having to wear a really crap uniform. I wonder if we are allowed makeup? At my school, if we had worn makeup we would have had our heads cut off. And put on the school gates as a warning to others.

But hahahahaha, I am on my own now.

I am flying solo.

I can cover myself in lipstick from head to foot if I feel like it.

Not that I will, actually, as I have only got one lipstick.

I need to get a lot more.

I wonder where Boots is in the village?

Dibdobs called me down for tea. I had changed into my jeans and a rib top and my Barely Pink lipstick. Live as you mean to go on, I say. In fact, I might go the whole hog and get some blusher.

Dibdobs had a frilly apron over her Brown Owl uniform when I went down into the kitchen. She was just dishing up sausages and she gave me a super-duper smile. I had no idea that teeth could be so . . . teethy.

She said, "They're local."

Does it matter that the sausages are local? I'm just going to eat them, not make friends and go to the cinema with them.

But she's only trying to be nice; this is how most people live. I think. But how would I know?

I smiled at her as I sat down in front of my sausages. And said, "Oh, goodie."

I've never said "Oh, goodie" in my life.

It feels good.

I may say it a lot and make it something I am notorious for.

Because when I am famous I will have to have a quirky personality.

I can't just rely on having sticky-out knees.

The door slammed open and a voice shouted, "I've

brought 'em back, I've got most of the worst off, but they'll need a good soak. Bye."

Dibdobs shouted, "Thanks, Nora."

The door slammed again and two toddlers shuffled into the kitchen.

Both with bowl haircuts.

Bowl hair with Play-Doh in it.

Dibdobs was busy at the stove and said over her shoulder, "Hello, boys, this is Tallulah."

They came and looked at me for a bit whilst I was chewing.

One said, "Goo-morning, did you hear me clenin my teeef?"

Um, it wasn't morning. And he didn't have any teeth except for one waggly one right at the front. And he didn't look like he would have that for long.

Mrs. Dobby was beside herself with joy.

"Tallulah, this is Max and Sam. Say hello, boys."

One started picking his nose and the other one, Max (or Sam), said, "They've gotten out, I've been feelin' for 'em but I can't find 'em."

Mrs. Dobby was getting a bit red in the face and her roundy glasses were steaming up, but she didn't raise her voice, she just said, "What is it you were feeling for to find, darling?"

Max, who had just been staring at me and waggling his loose tooth, piped up.

"Snails. Great big sjuuuge ones with sjuuuge shells."

I put my sausage to the side of my plate.

"We put them to seep."

Put them to seep?

Seep where?

They'd better not be seeping anywhere near me.

The boys stared at me all through my jelly and ice cream. And then, as a bit of light relief, Harold, Mr. Dobby, came home from his Christian table tennis.

He said, "Hello hello hello! Welcome welcome welcome. I'll just pop my table tennis bat in the bat drawer and I'll be with you."

He's jolly and beamy like Dibdobs and he's obviously where the twins get their looks from.

He also had a bowl haircut.

Perhaps Dibdobs has got a badge in "bowl cuts." I bet she has.

Despite his haircut, Harold is so happy. When he heard that the sausages were local he almost had to go and have a lie down, he was so thrilled. I like the Dobbinses already, but I don't know what to do with them. I'm not the dibdobdib jolly sort of person, I'm more the dark nobbly sort of person. But I did smile and nod a lot. Maybe they think that I am a bit shy?

That's good.

Shy is good.

I am going to be quite shy.

I will become known for my shyness.

And my quirky use of language, like saying "oh, goodie" or "yum yum." Or "yarooo!" Although I don't want to overdo it and make people think I'm a bit simple.

So, here I am in a squirrel room near a place called Grimbottom.

I put all my books on the shelves. *Wuthering Heights* is the set book for the course.

In my study notes it says:

How any human being could have attempted to write Wuthering Heights *without committing suicide before finishing two chapters is a mystery. It is a mixture of vulgar depravity and unnatural horrors.*

I was beginning to feel really sorry for myself and lonely when Dibdobs knocked on my door. She has brought me a mug of hot milk and, yarooo!, some slippers shaped like squirrels to make me "feel at home."

So she clearly thinks I live in a hole in a tree.

She said to me, "I hope you like them, Harold made them at his sewing class."

I said, "Oh yes, they're, well, they're very unusual . . . and spiffing."

Spiffing? Where did that come from? I am even

surprising myself with my quirky use of language.

I didn't have anything else to do, so after she had gone I tried my slippers on. You put your big toe into the snout and the ears stick out attractively at the sides. The tails nestle up the backs of your legs. Perhaps I should wear them to college for my first day, as a quirky fashion statement.

The zany, free world of a performer.

Hmmmmm. I could wear my false mustache AND the squirrel slippers on Monday. I could. If I wanted to make the girls laugh and the boys ignore me. The one thing I know about boys so far is that they don't like "fun" dressing in girls. I tried a cowboy hat on in Topshop and Connor practically wet himself.

I wonder what sort of boys will be at the college? Yeeha! A whole summer of boys. Painting, sculpting, dancing, leaping—leaping like gazelles pretending to be chasing birds. And of course, boys.

I am feeling nervous about Monday now. What if I am so rubbish at everything that I am asked to leave?

I was lying on my bed waggling my slippers around, preparing to tuck them up in bed with me, when I heard laughter from somewhere outside, nearly below my window, and a sort of shuffling and rustling.

A girl's voice grumpily said, "Oy, Cain, stop it. Are we officially going out or what?"

Then a boy's voice, quite deep and with a really strong accent, said, "There's no need to be such a mardy bum. I'm off, see you around."

The girl said, "When?"

And the boy's voice said, "I don't know, tha's getting on me nerves, I dint realize tha' were such a quakebottom. Why don't tha just hang around with the usual garyboys?"

A quakebottom?

Someone had got a trembling bottom?

I must see this.

I got off the bed and crawled to look through the window. It was very dark out there and I couldn't see much.

I heard the girl say, "Oy, Cain, wait for me!"

Then there was a sudden loud fluttering of wings and flash of white and a horrible screech like something had been killed. And illuminated in the moonlight, I saw an eerie snowy barn owl fly up into a tree near my window. It settled on the branch facing me and I could see a mouse. Dangling out of its beak.

The owl looked at me and blinked really slowly. Then it shut its eyes completely. The mouse started disappearing, bit by bit. The owl was swallowing the mouse whole. Head first. And having a little snooze at the same time.

Crikey.

My notes are bloody right. This is a place of vulgar depravity and unnatural horrors. And that's just Cain.

Summer of Love

How CAN IT BE foggy in July?

Maybe it's not fog, it's the mists coming in from the moors. Oooohhhhhh. The moors, the mysterious dark moors.

I've been awake since sunrise but the sun hasn't risen. There was hooting going on all night.

I don't remember that being mentioned in the extensively illustrated Dother Hall brochure.

I got my brochure out again:

Heckmondwhite has its own "zany" cosmopolitan atmosphere.

Oooh, that sounds good. I'd better get dressed and have a look round Heckmondwhite and check out its "zany" atmosphere. I only saw the village green last night. The high street and Boots must be farther on.

I looked in the mirror. Yes, there I am. It's me again. This northern light certainly makes my eyes look green. Not just a bit light brown like some people have and say they are green.

Is that a good thing?

I've got the same coloring as my mum—very dark hair. She says it's from the Irish side. I asked her which side my knees were from and she said, "the circus side," which she thought was hilarious.

Why am I on this course heading for the West End? I didn't really think I would get on it. To be perfectly honest, I've only been in a couple of school plays. The last one was my own special version of *Alice in Wonderland* and I cast myself as a playing card. So if there are any standing-around-stiffly parts going, I'll be in like a ferret up a trouser leg.

I've put my hair in a ponytail and I've got mascara on. What can I do about being so pale? I know, I can pop into Boots, because they are open on Sundays, and see if they do any "cheeky" products.

Coming out the door, Dibdobs said, "I think the sun's trying to get out."

I smiled at her and said, "Top of the morning to you!"

It seems to be brightening up. The fog has cleared so

now you can see the sheep, and over there, some sheep and a pig. No sign of people, unless they are crouching down behind the sheep.

I'll go to the top of the lane and explore the village before I go to the high street.

Two rough-looking, dark-haired lads were by the bus stop, arguing about something. One of them got the other round the neck, yelling, "Take that back, tha great gary-boy."

And the other one kicked him in the shin and then took off, shouting back, "Come and get me, tha manky pillock, I'll brain you!"

It's charming being in the country.

I wonder if one of them is that Cain boy. Who would call a person Cain? Wasn't he the boy in the Bible that killed his own brother?

Cain. You might as well call him "Rottenhead" and have done with it.

OK, well here I am at the village green and there's the village hall next to the pub, and then on this side is the grocer's store, church, and bus stop. I suppose the road to the main shopping bit is the one that goes off round the back of the pub.

The pub is called The Blind Pig. It's got a sign with a pig on it. The piggy has dark glasses on and a walking stick in its trotter. Must be an olde Yorkshire story about a pig that saved the village single-handedly from the Vikings, even though it was blind.

Actually, it wouldn't be single-handedly, it would be single-trotteredly.

As I turned down the lane to the shops, a girl about my age came out of The Blind Pig. She had a mass of curly hair and a cute sticky-up nose.

She smiled at me and said, "Hello, do you live here?"

I smiled back and said, "No, I'm Tallulah and I've come to Yorkshire by mistake."

She laughed and crinkled her nose up. She had a very gurgling, hiccupping sort of laugh. She said, "My name's Vaisey and I'm starting the performing arts summer school at Dother Hall."

Hooray! Someone else on the planet besides Brown Owls and bowl-headed people. Vaisey was staying at The Blind Pig because her bed wasn't ready at the school.

I said, "Did you come with anyone, or do you know people there?"

She shook her hair. "Not yet, but I think it's going to be great, don't you? I feel a touch of the tap dancing coming on, I am so excited. The landlord of the pub says that they call it 'Dither Hall' in the village and that it's all scarves and tambourines up there."

I said, "Um . . . who's the landlord?"

At which point, a big, red-faced man in tweed breeches came out and looked at us.

"Oh . . . I see, another of you. Are you breeding?"

He shouted back into the pub, "Ruby, I said this would 'appen. The 'artists' are breeding already, there'll be bloody hundreds of them by tomorrow. All miming their way to the bus stop."

He went off in the direction of the village hall, laughing like a rusty goose.

A girl of about ten popped her head out of the pub door to look at us. She had pigtails and gap teeth and freckles, and a sweet little face.

She said in a broad accent, "Ullo, I'm Ruby. Who are you?"

I said, "I'm Tallulah."

Ruby laughed and laughed and then said, "That's a mad name. I think I'll just call tha Loobylullah for short."

I laughed as well. I felt sort of nice that she had made up a special name for me. I said to them both, "I was going to go to the shops. Do you fancy coming?"

Vaisey said, "Yes, that would be cool, let's go. Which way is it?"

I said, "It must be down this road because I know there is only the village green thing here."

Ruby was just looking at us.

I said, "Are you not coming?"

She said, "No, I'll leave it."

"See you later then."

Ruby said, "Yep."

Me and Vaisey set off down the road and passed the back of The Blind Pig and its outbuildings.

Then we came to a line of cottages and a barn.

Vaisey said, "Which do you like best: cappuccino or hot chocolate? I think I will have hot chocolate. . . ."

And that's when we saw more sheep. Fields of them, stretching as far as the eye could see.

Oh no, of course I am exaggerating, there was a sign as well and it said:

Blubberhouse Sewage Works 10 miles

We were back at The Blind Pig two minutes later and Ruby was sitting on the wall eating a bag of crisps.

She said, "Did you not go to the shops?"

We shook our heads.

Ruby said quite kindly, "Have you two ever bin in the country before?"

We shook our heads.

Ruby said, "The woolly things are sheep. See thee later, I'm off to the pie-eating contest, my dad's in it."

Vaisey and me decided to make the best of things by looking round what there was of the village. I'll give you a thumbnail sketch of the high spots.

The post office. What we could see through the window: stamps, ten "amusing" birthday cards, Sellotape.

The village shop. Pies, milk, tea bags, paint, and a selection of boiled sweets.

I won't bother you with the low spots.

As we passed, we could hear loud cheering and heckling from the village hall. It was decorated with a banner that said: *PIE EATING.*

A loud voice bellowed from inside. It sounded like Ruby. "Come on, Dad, get it down you! Only twenty to go!!!"

I looked at Vaisey. She said, "Do you want to see my room?"

The pub smelled all beery when we went in. It didn't have what you would call a "cosmopolitan atmosphere." It had a dartboard-and-skittles atmosphere.

It looked like one of those pubs that you see in scary old films. You know, when two lost travelers are on the moors. Suddenly a thunderstorm breaks. They are soaking and the lightning is crackling across the sky. Then they hear something terrible howling. And as they walk on, the howling gets nearer. A flash of lightning illuminates a slathering monstrous dog with fangs. And they start running, and the beast starts running, and one falls over and then . . . Heavens to Betsy, they see lights! And hear a piano. The welcoming lights of an old inn. The sign creaks backward and forward in the howling wind. A flash of lightning illuminates the sign.

It reads, *The Blind Pig.*

Anyway, that is what The Blind Pig was like. I was glad the landlord was out eating pies.

There were pictures of Ruby's dad all over the walls. Mostly with dead things that he had shot. Foxes, stags, deer. Chickens. A cow. Surely he hadn't shot a cow? In each one he was standing with his shotgun and his foot on whatever poor thing he had shot. There was even one of him with one foot on a pie. Underneath it said:

Ted Barraclough, Champion Pie-Eater:
22 steak-and-kidney and 4 pork.

We went up the steep stairs to Vaisey's room. It had dark oak beams and slanting wooden floors, it was so old. Yorkshire people seem obsessed with wood. There is very little city loft-living style around here. Where are all the shiny surfaces?

Vaisey prattled about her family as we looked through her things. Two brothers and a sister. Dogs, two budgies, both called Joey. Ordinary everyday legs. She told me she could sing and dance a bit and that she had played Titania in *A Midsummer Night's Dream* and tap-danced in the forest bit.

Tap dancing? Would I have to tap-dance? I can't.

Butterflies started biffing each other in my tummy. Should I have gone with Connor and taken my chances with the bug sandwiches?

To take my mind off tomorrow I said, "Vaisey, have you got a boyfriend?"

She went bright red. And twitched her nose, like a mop-haired bunny.

Then she got up from the bed and went to the window, put her hand to her forehead, and whispered, "Aahhh, *l'amour, l'amour, pour quoi? C'est une* mystery."

I said to her, "Um . . . did you just say in French, 'love, love, for why, it's a mystery'?"

She shook her curls and laughed sadly.

"It was a line from a piece we did last term at school. I was a suicidal nun."

Gosh.

I didn't think I'd mention my playing-card experience just yet.

"So does that mean you've been dumped by a boy?"

And Vaisey said, "No, it means it's a mystery because I haven't snogged a boy—yet."

Vaisey and I have decided that we will try and have a joint Summer of Love.

Just then I heard Mr. Barraclough coming in shouting, "Pie! Pie! Pie!" Time to go home for tea.

Dibdobs has been face painting with the boys. She was a butterfly. It was quite a scary sight. Then the twins came in.

She was not as scary as the bowl-headed owls.

After tea—yes, it was local pies, Harold couldn't believe his luck—the Dobbinses thought a game of Cluedo might be fun, but I said, "I think I should get to bed early for my first day at college."

Harold said, "At quarter to six?"

I think even they thought that quarter to six was early by anybody's standards.

I gave my artistic laugh and also threw in some quirky language for good measure. "Lawks-a-mercy, no! I'm going to have a long bath and . . ."

I looked shyly down. Which is pretty impressive to have done artistic laugh, quirky language, and shyness all in the space of ten seconds.

I said, "I need to prepare myself. You know, limber up . . . my artistic . . . muscles. Soak up the atmosphere, maybe read *Jane Eyre*. Anyway, have a lovely evening guessing who bludgeoned who to death."

I left Dibdobs stuffing the insane brothers into their nightshirts.

I've painted my nails a midnight-blue color and I think I will wear mostly black tomorrow. To blend in. It will be funny not wearing a uniform to go to school. And to wear a bit of makeup.

I stayed for ages in the bath. Some of the girls at my school at home were really "mature" for their age. Kate and Siobhan had bras. And a few of them were getting hair under their arms.

If you don't get bosomy bits by a certain age does that mean you won't ever get them? I read in one of the magazines that handling them makes them grow.

Maybe I will try rubbing mine about a bit with the soap. To encourage them.

Half an hour later.

My arms are killing me.

Even if my lady chest bits don't grow I am going to have strong arms. If there is a trapeze class I will be very good at it.

Also I will have very clean lady chest bits.

When I came out of the bathroom the twins were staring at me from the hall. Sucking on their dodies. They're not tall enough to look through the keyhole of the bathroom door, are they? They couldn't have seen me making my lady chest bits grow, could they?

I went off to my room.

I could chart my progress.

Maybe do a bit of measuring.

You know, legs: eight feet high. Lady chest bits: one inch each.

I wonder if I can find another word for my nonchest bits . . . ?

Norkers?

Ping-Pong balls in a string bag?

Honkers?

Corkers?

Actually, I quite like "corkers." Well, I would if I actually had any corkers.

But I am in fact corkerless.

I went into my squirrel room and was just looking for a book to read when the door creaked open and revealed the twins. I don't know why they like to look at me so much. I looked back at them and then Dibdobs came bustling in and said, "Boys, there you are! What do you say at nightie-night time to Tallulah?"

Sam said, "Bogie."

Dibdobs went a bit red and she said, "No, that's a silly word, isn't it? We say 'Night night, Tallulah.' You boys say it now. Night night, Tallulah. . . ."

The boys just stared, then Max said, "Ug oo."

And turned and went off.

Dibdobs said, "Yes, that's right, but say, 'Ug oo, Tallulah.'"

Sam said, "Ug oo."

And Dibdobs said, "Tallulah."

And Sam said, "Bogie."

Dibdobs ushered him out. "Silly, silly word. Don't say it anymore. Let's have a little story. Shall we read about Thomas the Tank Engine?"

"Bogie."

I'm reading *Jane Eyre* tonight. It's not *Wuthering Heights* but it has the same Yorkshire grimness. I've got up to the bit when Jane goes back to see Mr. Rochester at Thornfield Hall and it is burnt to smithereens and he is blind.

Yarooo!

And it is probably raining and foggy.

The Brontës are what you might call "a laugh."

Hang on a minute.

Dother Hall looks like Thornfield Hall.

The hooting has started again.

Your feet will bleed

WHEN I WOKE UP I was all atremble. I could hardly get my squirrel slippers on. I'm going to open my note from Georgia to calm me down. A bit of grown-up advice from someone older and wiser. Who has snogged.

> Dear Tallulah,
> Remember. A boy in the hand is worth two on the bus.
> Luuurve Georgia x

What bus?

I washed my hair and it's still damp, but at least it's swishy. Swishy hair can get you a long way.

The Dobbinses gave me a family hug and I went off to meet Vaisey by the post office. It was a bright, sunny day and she was wearing a little red skirt, leggings, a red denim jacket, and a cheeky little hat.

She said, "I didn't sleep much, did you?"

I said, "No, I had this dream that I went onstage and realized that I'd forgotten my knees, so my legs were all floppy, and I was flopping around."

Vaisey looked at me.

As we walked along the woodland path to Dother Hall, we saw another sign pointing in the opposite direction. It said:

Woolfe Academy for Young Men

Cor, love a duck. And also Lawks-a-mercy. I said that inwardly, but outwardly I said, "Blimey, and also, what larks, it looks like there's going to be tons of boys around."

Vaisey's face went as red as her little hat.

And I must say the butterflies were now playing Ping-Pong in my tummy. But what if the boys were like Cain and those village boys? Sort of grunting instead of talking.

And moody.

And possibly violent.

It only took us twenty minutes to walk to the Hall. It was a lovely walk if you like baaing. Which I sort of did this morning.

Then we rounded a corner and saw before us the

"magnificent center of artistry," Dother Hall. I couldn't help noticing its fine Edwardian front and the fact that its roof was on fire.

As we looked up at the flames and smoke a figure emerged onto the roof in between the high chimney pots.

I said to Vaisey, "Bloody hell, it's Mrs. Rochester. Bagsie I'm not Jane Eyre, I don't want to get married to some blind bloke who shouts a lot."

Vaisey said, "It can't really be Mrs. Rochester, can it?"

I said, "Well, you say that, but it all adds up, doesn't it? We're in Yorkshire on some moors at a big house, the roof's on fire, and someone, who may or may not have been banged up in the attic for years, has just come out onto the roof. I'm only stating the obvious. Who else could it be?"

Then we noticed that "Mrs. Rochester" was wearing a mackintosh and carrying a fire extinguisher. And she started putting the fire out with foam.

After the fire was out Mrs. Rochester disappeared amongst the chimneys.

We went up the steep front steps into a huge entrance hall where about twenty girls were giggling and shuffling about. It's funny being in a place where you don't know one single person. Well, apart from a person you only met the day before.

Vaisey said, "That girl over there by the bust of Nelson

is standing in first position from ballet."

Never mind about ballet positions, where were all the boys?

Suddenly a woman in a pinafore dress, with her hair in a mad bun, burst through the door. She had a clipboard.

Over the noise she yelled, *"Guten Tag, Fräulein, und Willkommen."*

Then she started laughing. Well, honking, really, to be accurate.

She said, "The joke is, girls, I'm not German. You don't have to be crazy to work here, but it helps!!!!!"

And she was off hooting again.

"So, let's get to know each other. I am Gudrun Sachs and I pretty much run the place! Well, I am the principal's secretary. First of all, I want to take your names and tick you off!! No, no, not tell you off, just put a little tick next to your names. Off we jolly well *gehen*."

She pointed to Vaisey. "You, dear, name, dear?"

Vaisey went red and said, "Vaisey Davenport."

Gudrun did a big tick on her list.

Then she pointed her pen at me.

I said, "Tallulah Casey."

Gudrun said, "Oh begorrah, begorrah, to be sure."

Crumbs.

She went round the group, and I tried to remember some of the girls; there was Jo and Flossie and Pippy and Becka; Honey, I think; I do remember Milly and Tilly because they rhymed. But unfortunately I was so busy thinking that their names rhymed I can't remember who is who.

As we were being ticked off, Mrs. Rochester came barging through, covered in foam. Gudrun said, "Everything back to normal in the fire department, Bob?"

Mrs. Rochester, otherwise known as Bob, said, "The fire's out but I've singed my ponytail in the process."

He had actually. Well, not so much singed as burnt half of it off. The ends were all frazzled.

Gudrun said, "Perhaps if you trimmed off the singed bits it could be more of a . . . a . . . bob?"

Then she started chortling with laughter. "Do you see what I did there . . . ? Bob is called Bob and then I made a wordplay about his ponytail."

After he'd gone, Gudrun said, "Bob is our technician-cum-handyman. We have this very funny joke about Bob. If we are looking for him, someone might say, 'Bob about?' and that is the signal for the rest of us to start, you know, 'Bob-ing about.'"

And she started jumping up and down and bobbing about.

"Do you see? Taking the expression 'bob about' literally. Do you see?"

We all just looked at her.

★ ★ ★

As she led us into the main hall, I said to Vaisey, "Where are the boys? Where is Martin and his tiny instrument?"

Vaisey said, "I don't know, perhaps he was just a model."

I looked at her. "What, you mean, made out of Plasticine?"

Vaisey said, "No, you know, not really a student, but a model pretending to be a student."

I didn't know what to say.

We went to sit down.

The hall had a stage at the end of it with a film screen set up. I sat on the end of a row, and Vaisey was next to a small black-haired girl. She had black shiny eyes as well. A bit like a human conker.

Vaisey and I said hello to her, and she said, "I'm Jo. I know you think I'm quite short, but I'm deceptively strong."

Um.

She said, "I am."

I said, "I didn't say you weren't."

Jo said, "No, but because I'm short you're thinking, she can't really be that strong. She might be quite strong for a short-arse, but she's not ordinarily strong."

What was she going on about? I said, "I hadn't noticed that you were short anyway."

She said, "Well I am."

I said, "I'm not saying you're not, I am just saying that

I hadn't noticed, so if I hadn't noticed that might mean that . . ."

She stood up and I said, "Jesus, Mary, and Joseph, you are short, aren't you? Are you sure you're not crouching down?"

Jo said, "You see, you see! You do think I'm short."

I said, "Well, you are. Compared to me, I mean. But then I'm too tall, really."

She'd gone a bit red now and said, "All right, but you just have a go at pushing me over, then we'll see who's short."

Vaisey said, "I don't think that . . . pushing and so on is . . ."

Jo said to me, "Go on."

I said, "I don't want to, I might hurt you."

She said, "That is what you think, but you just wait. Honestly, you'll get a surprise."

I thought I would give her a bit of a shove to be polite. Unfortunately, I did it just as she was turning round to put her bag on her seat. I didn't push her very hard, but she still careered sideways over two empty chairs and headfirst into a big girl's lap. Who said, "Oy."

When Jo got up her face was nearly as red as Vaisey's hat. But she had pluck, I would give her that. She smoothed down her hair and said, "I wasn't ready, try again."

I said, "Look, can we just leave it that I think you are really strong and—"

She said, "You're scared you'll hurt yourself."

I said, "Oh, all right."

This time she tensed herself. I stepped back to get a proper run up and said to Vaisey, "Would you mind moving, Vaisey, so I can knock this person, who I have only just met, into the middle of next week!"

At which point I felt a hand on my shoulder. I looked round and up to see a tall thin woman in a cloak. She said, "And what is your name?" And not in a nice, interested way.

I said, "Tallulah Casey."

And she got out a little notepad, and said out loud as she wrote, "Ta-llu-lah Caaaaasee-y."

Then she shut the notepad with a snap and said, "Now let me tell you my name. It's Doctor Lightowler."

I was tempted to say, "Aaaaah Dooooooctor Liiiiightowwwwler," but I didn't.

She threw her cloak back over her shoulders and said, "I don't know what sort of school you are from, but here at Dother Hall, we do not fight."

I said, "But she asked me if I would push her over. I was only being polite."

Dr. Lightowler looked at me. A bit like the mouse-eating owl, actually.

Spooky.

The doctor said, "We shall come to know each other very well, Ta-llu-lah Caaa-sey."

And she didn't seem to mean getting to know each other in a friendy-wendy way.

As she went off, Jo said, "Well, I thought that went well, didn't you? I think she secretly likes you. But don't worry, I will protect you from her."

And she put her arm in mine. I think things were going quite well. In a friendy-wendy way.

A funny clock chimed somewhere and a door to the right of the stage opened. A woman in white suede cowboy boots and a fringed jacket walked slowly to the front of the stage and looked out intently.

We looked back at her.

She looked back at us.

Then, finally, in a throaty posh voice she said, "Welcome, fellow artistes. You see how I have got your attention. I have made this stage my own. In a few short weeks, we will teach you the same skills. You too will fill the stage."

I nudged Vaisey, but she seemed to be hypnotized by the stage-filling idea.

The woman went on, "I am Sidone Beaver. Not Sid-one Beaver, or Sid-ony Beaver but Sid-o-nee Beaver, principal of Dother Hall. Here to guide you to the theater of dreams. Think of me less as a headmistress and more like . . . the keeper of the gateway . . . of your flight to . . . the stars."

Jeepers creepers.

Sid-o-nee was still filling the stage.

"I know you sit before me, young, nervous. You think, how could I ever be like her? But I can still remember my own beginnings in this crazy, heartbreaking, cruel, wonderful, mad, mad world of art. The highs, the lows . . . let me not mince words, let me not blind you with dreams. There is no easy passage, no free lunch. This is a tough path. . . . Your feet will bleed before you experience the golden slippers of applause!"

We looked at our feet.

Soon to be bleeding.

Sidone went on, "By the end of these few short weeks, some of you will be the 'chosen' and some of you will be the 'unchosen.'"

What did that mean?

When Sidone left the stage we were shown a film of students working at different projects at Dother Hall.

Ooh, look, here were students tap-dancing, and some sword fighting in the woods. Students making a papier-mâché sculpture.

Jo whispered, "Why are they making a big stool?"

Vaisey said, "It's an elephant."

There was one photo of students dressed in black jumpsuits with painted white faces, looking at a motorbike.

I said to Vaisey, "What are they supposed to be?"

She shrugged.

The caption said at the end: *Students produce a clown*

version of Grease.

But funnily enough, although there were one or two shots of male teachers—oh, and Bob banging at stuff with a wrench—there were no boys around.

Until right at the end.

At last.

There was Martin making his tiny instrument. I elbowed Vaisey. "Look, there's Martin with his lute!"

There was a break afterward. I felt quite dazed. "Chosen"—"unchosen"—"bleeding feet"—"golden slippers of applause"?

We followed the signs to the café. Vaisey, me, and Jo.

Jo said, "I'm really, really excited, aren't you? I didn't sleep a wink last night, well, it wasn't the excitement of course, it was because of the whole dorm thing."

Vaisey nodded. "I'd quite like to see the dorm, actually. I wonder if . . ."

Jo said, "Oh, you weren't here last night, were you?"

Vaisey said, "No. I was supposed to be here, but my bed wasn't quite ready, or something."

Jo laughed grimly. "Be glad you weren't in it, because that's where the roof came in—over your bed. Bob nailed up an old blanket to keep the bats out and I think that is what caught fire. I'm not surprised, really; when Milly switched on her bedside lamp, it was giving off sparks. There was a dead pigeon in the loo. Maybe electrocuted."

As we got our tea and biccies I said to the other girls, "I don't want to go on about Martin and his lute, but, where is Martin and his lute? And where are Martin's mates?"

We looked at Jo.

Jo said, "Ahh, you mean Martin and his mates. Well, Dother Hall used to be mixed, but there was some sort of incident involving a game called 'twenty-five in a duvet cover' and since then boys are banned."

I said, "What a swizz. Still, at least there's Woolfe Academy."

We asked Jo if she knew anything about it.

She said, "No, but I would like to. At home, I'm at an all-girls school."

After break we were taken on a tour of the theater department by Bob. I think he has given his ponytail a quick trim.

He was wearing a T-shirt that said *Fat men are harder to kidnap*.

Bob said, "Sit down on the floor. Mr. de Courcy will be with you in a minute. Don't play around with the lights, dudes."

As he went out, we saw that his T-shirt had *ROCK* on the back and that he was wearing very low-slung jeans with a belt that had all sorts of hammers and stuff hanging off it. And unfortunately, it was pulling his trousers down. I didn't want to look but something pale was peeping out under his T-shirt. I think it was his bottom.

One of the other girls said, "It's theater in the round."

I didn't like to ask what that was. Only round people are allowed to be in it? Probably.

The girl who had said "theater in the round" was the big girl who Jo had fallen into the lap of. So perhaps that is why she was so *au fait* with theater in the round. She had thick-framed glasses on and dark hair in a ponytail with a big, clunky fringe. So that you couldn't see if she had eyebrows or not. She was looking at me.

I don't know why, I had my knees covered up.

I looked back. I was trying not to blink.

She didn't blink either.

I had accidentally entered a no-blinking competition. On my first day at performing arts college. Things were hotting up.

Then the girl made her eyes go upwards so you could just see the white bits. Like in *Night of the Zombies*. It made me laugh. And that was the official end of the no-blinking competition. We shook hands and she said, "Hello. You've got green eyes."

I said, "I know."

She said, "I know you know, but now I know."

And I said, "I know."

Two minutes later it seemed that everyone was chatting to one another. The zombie girl is called Florence, although her mates call her Flossie, and she is from Blackpool.

I said, "Do you go on the pier and get candy, Flossie?"

She said, "Do you do that a lot?"

I said, "What?"

And she said, "Make really, really crap jokes?"

Jo and Vaisey said, "Yes."

And she said, "I think I might like you quite a lot."

A few people were doing handstands against the wall and the volume had gone up by a million when the door banged open to reveal a fat bloke. (I say things as I see things, and I couldn't see the door anymore, so I know I am right about the fatness.)

The bloke had little roundy cheeks, you know, the ones that look like there is a snack concealed in each one, for later. He was wearing a suit with a waistcoat. And a bow tie. And he had tiny sort of piggy eyes. Or maybe they weren't really piggy eyes, they were just squashed up by his cheeks.

He clapped his pudgy hands together. *"Mes enfants, mes enfants!! Tranquil! Tranquil!"*

Everyone did go quiet, but I don't think it was because he had said "be quiet" in French. I think it was the sheer size of his trousers.

He said, "I am Monty de Courcy, I have the privilege and the honor to teach you the wonders of theater.

"The magic of the-ater.

"The language of the-a-ter.

"You and I shall eat, live, breathe the the-a-ter. Let's to work!"

I don't think I can go a whole thummer without boyth

IN THE AFTERNOON WE were told that we could have the rest of the day to explore, but first we would be given our assignment for tomorrow.

When we arrived in the entrance hall, Sidone was playing a cello dressed in a velvet trouser suit. Sidone, not the cello.

Monty de Courcy entered wearing a top hat and stopped in front of us.

Was he wearing eye liner?

He took the top hat off and put his finger to his lips.

Then he shook the hat.

Had he got a rabbit in there?

He beckoned to us, so we shuffled over.

Jo said, "Sir, shall we take—"

Monty shook his head and put his finger over his lips again.

Jo said very quietly, "But, sir, shall we take—"

Then he started winking and tapping his nose and raising his eyebrows all at the same time.

Then, he came over to me and pointed a finger into the hat. Oh . . . there were envelopes in there.

Vaisey looked at me and shrugged. I shrugged back. We all shrugged.

Finally Monty lost his rag silently and handed the envelopes out himself.

On the front of the envelope it said: *Open me just before you go to sleep. Dream on the contents.*

We walked past Sidone, who was still playing the cello, and as we passed she said in a whispering voice, "Girls, my girls . . . soft, soft, what dreams are these?"

She looked at us.

And raised her eyebrows.

I have no idea. What dreams? What soft?

We popped to the loos to find that Bob had pinned a notice up in there. It said:

Listen up, dudes, Dother Hall is seriously green.

THINK: Finished your bath? Wait! Why not rinse out your smalls in the bathwater? Bob

Vaisey went red because Bob had written "smalls."

We all got together on the grass to eat our sandwiches. I was lying on my back with one leg over the other, looking up at the sky. I'm beginning to feel really great now. New friends, freedom, and everything. I am ready to start filling my tights. I'm not a little girl anymore. I am trembling on the edge of womanhood. As the rest of them were chomping away, I said, "I feel like I'm really growing up now."

And I uncrossed my legs and unfortunately kicked Flossie in the back of her head. She nearly choked on her tuna surprise.

Jo said, "Lullah, are you starting to grow up from the waist down? Your legs are about a million feet long."

I said, "I know, I really hate my legs."

Jo sat up. "You've got cracking legs, really long. Look at mine."

We looked at hers. I thought they were nice legs, actually, with dimples in her knees. Not long—well, short, to be frank.

Vaisey said, "Look at my bum, look how it sticks out. And if I jump up and down and shake at the same time, it waggles about."

Jo said, "I think it's horrid how everything is to do with

looks and it doesn't count if you are a nice person. Why should it matter what your legs are like?"

I said, "I agree with you, but . . . look at these!"

I rolled up my trousers and let my legs be free and wild in the summer air.

They looked at them.

Flossie said, "My cousin Jenet has legs like yours, and my auntie took her to a doctor."

I said, "Am I going to like this story?"

Flossie said, "Shhh, I'm talking. Anyway, the doctor said Jenet was like a racehorse."

I said, "What, she had four really long, thin legs?"

Flossie came and sat on me. I think she is what is known in showbiz as "violent."

She said, "No, what he meant was that she will grow into her legs. And you will grow into yours and then that will be good. And you will stop moaning."

Vaisey was pulling at her hair, which, and I don't mean this unkindly, did look like a really badly knitted hat.

She said, "And you've got very attractive hair, not like mine."

I know I should have said, "No, no, no, no you've got lovely hair!" But really I wanted to hear more about mine first. So I said, "How do you mean 'attractive hair'?"

Flossie said, "You know very well what she means. She means you've got very attractive hair."

I said, in a shy surprised voice, "Have I?"

Flossie said, "Yes, you have, but you've got very bad acting skills. You KNOW that your hair is all glossy and black as a hearth."

I couldn't help doing a secret tee-hee.

And Jo said, "And you've got green eyes. If you wanted, you could be like a traffic light or something, they are so green."

I felt a bit cheered up.

I said, in a fit of general loving the worldness, "I think we are all very, very lovely."

Honey came and sat with us. She walks slowly and softly, so that you don't notice her coming. Not in a creepy "I'm going to rob your handbag" way, just in a softy way. It's nice.

Honey seems just like her name. Sort of golden and smoothy. Her skin is golden and her hair is thick and gold. And she has quite big corkers. And she's sweet, just like honey made by bees. Except that that kind of honey doesn't have a lisp.

"I know I have a lithp. I lithp and I like it. And boyth theem to like it too!"

Vaisey had got interested now. She said, "Honey, do you know about boys? Have you got a boyfriend?"

Honey said, "Oh yeth, I've got two on the go, actually. Thafety in numberth, my mum thayth. I don't think I can go a whole thummer without boyth."

After lunch, we walked off toward Heckmondwhite. Vaisey, Jo, Flossie, and I were slightly ahead of the others. Flossie said, "Oooh, look, a couple of jolly farmers in their fields. One of them is cheerily waving his stick at us. Would it be a stick or a crook? It's not a gun, is it?"

I said, "Oh, what larks, it's the grumpy bloke I accidentally kicked on the train."

As we ambled along, Jo said, "Do you think that Honey really has got two boyfriends?"

Vaisey said, "She seems a bit more 'mature' than us, more experienced, don't you think?"

I said, "I've had my bottom felt."

Flossie said, "Who by? Not your mum?"

I said, "No, it was an actual boy."

Vaisey said, "Was it nice?"

I said, "Well, not really, because he pretended it wasn't his hand, it was his kitbag."

Jo said, "I've had my bra undone through my T-shirt."

I said, "Great balls of fire, who did that?"

Jo said, "I don't know which one, because they all bombed off on their bikes before I could see."

Vaisey said, "My cousin put an ice cube down the front of my T-shirt and then offered to get it out for me."

I said, "Is that it then? A maybe fondling of a bum, a hit-and-run undone thing, and an ice cube incident?"

Flossie said, "No, not quite . . ."

We turned to look at her.

She said, "Well, this is how it happened. It was a hot steamy night, you know, those kind of nights when you feel restless. You want something to happen and you don't quite know what? Like you were in a play set in Mississippi and you can hear the damn crickets. Going on and on."

Jo said, "They don't play cricket in Mississippi."

Flossie said, "Someone kill her while I carry on."

We stopped walking.

Flossie took off her glasses. And loosened her hair and tossed it about. Then she stretched her arms above her head and sighed and went on in a sort of Texan drawl. "Now y'all know how damn hoooooottttt it can get in high summer. To get some air, I decided to peg out some washing. My smalls, actually. Although I hadn't washed them in dirty bathwater. What a fool I feel now."

I said, "Will you get on with it?"

Flossie went on in a quiet voice. "I was peggin' out some of my pants when I saw a couple of young fellas watchin' me. One of them was quite handsome. When I turned round, he ducked behind a bush. I thought, ah, he's kinda shy. So I kinda half smiled in the direction of the bush and set off, slowly into the house."

Flossie mimed picking up a washing basket and sashaying down the road. "Then I heard a rustlin' behind me. Aah, I thought, now he will say 'Miss Flossie, you are so goddam beautiful.' But the rustlin' was followed by

49

pingin' and one of those boys was wearin' my smalls on his head. And ran off wearin' them."

When we got to Heckmondwhite it took us the usual minute and a half to go round the village. Some of the girls pretended to be interested in the cards in the post office. But it is very hard to be interested in ten copies of a card that has a picture of that fat bloke from *Little Britain* on the front. And you open it and it says, "I want that one."

Vaisey wanted to go home and go to bed and start dreaming on whatever our assignment is. Which I think is slightly cheating because it's only six o'clock. The other girls had to be back at Dother Hall for tea, so I slumped off home to the Dobbinses' house.

I am exhausted. I could hardly eat my ham sandwiches. And trifle. And Eccles cake. The Dobbinses were on rope-weaving duty and so they went out after tea. Dibdobs gave me a little huglet as she went.

"Come and do a bit of weaving, Tallulah, it's fun! Mr. Barraclough often brings us ginger beer and does impressions. He did a very funny one of a ferret up his trouser leg last time."

I said I would pass.

In my squirrel room, I'm glad I'm not in the dorm with a blanket over my head. It's hot and sticky, even though it's after nine o'clock. Maybe there's going to be a violent thunderstorm. I've done my corkies-rubbing exercises and I can't say I can see any difference yet. Although my arms look slightly bigger.

Right, I am going to open my envelope to find out about the assignment for tomorrow:

> *Tomorrow we begin our big adventure. Be prepared. Sleep. Bring comfortable workout clothes.*
> *And now . . . think of a word, or words, that sum you up.*
> *Dream on it.*
> *Bring it to the college tomorrow.*

A word or words that sum me up?

I lay in the squirrel bed thinking.

Nobbly?

Long?

Corkieless?

Oh, that's attractive, isn't it? In conclusion, I am a long, nobbly person with no corkers.

Help!

Everything is so different here. And even though the girls are only messing about, I know for a fact that Honey plays the piano, and so does Vaisey. And Vaisey has been a suicidal nun.

Should I drop that thing that Cousin Georgia said about Norwegian art into the conversation? What did she say it was called? Sled-werk.

There must be something I am good at. Besides being able to get stuff down from the top shelf.

I can't sleep, it's no use. I'm too hot. And I'm too worried (and nobbly and long).

I'll think about something else. What, though?

Oh, I know. Dad sent me a book through the post from wherever he is. Anyway, it turns out to be a James Bond book. In his note, Dad said I would learn a lot from it. He says he did.

I'll just open it randomly.

Oh, here's some stuff about boy things. James Bond and Honeychile. Ooh, that's funny, isn't it? Being a bit like Honey.

It was unbearably hot in the hotel bedroom in Jamaica. Outside, the geckos and parakeets were settling down noisily for the night.

I'll just have to try and imagine the noise of the parakeets above the baaing and grunting outside my window.

Honeychile got up from the bed and took off all her clothes. She went and stood next to the window.

Crumbs.

*Bond went across to her and took a breast in each
hand. But still she looked away from him out the
window.*

"Not now," she said in a low voice.

Is that what you're supposed to do?

I went to the open window. And when I looked down I
saw a boy and girl, um, snogging. The girl had her back to
me and her arms wrapped round the boy's neck. I couldn't
see his face. I wondered if it was like in the James Bond
book and he was holding one of her breasts in each hand?

If he was, she would turn her head away in a minute
and say, "Not now." I couldn't see because of the angle. . . .
And that's when she snuggled into his shoulder and he
looked up at my window.

He looked at me.

I looked at him.

I was like a rabbit in a headlight.

Maybe I can pretend I'm just drawing the curtains.

There aren't any curtains.

Perhaps I could pretend to be cleaning the windows.

I haven't got a duster.

I could use the sleeve of my jimjams.

Good. Good idea.

Creative.

Improvise cleaning a window.

He was still looking at me as I started cleaning the window with my sleeve.

Then he winked at me.

How disgusting.

To be snogging one girl and winking at another.

What sort of person did that?

He is like a wild animal. A winking, snogging, wild animal.

Then the girl said, "Oy, Cain, what are you looking at?"

I shut the window quickly.

Cain. Why is he always underneath my window?

We first learn to fill our tights

I WOKE UP EARLY THE NEXT DAY. I'd been dreaming that I had a bra made out of soap. It slipped off when I did my special audition dance and everyone laughed.

I am going to tie my hair up and wear a hat. Cain won't recognize me again out of my jimjams, will he?

Oh Lord, he has seen me in my jimjams. Watching him snog.

I went down to breakfast and the Dobbinses were all as cheerful as people who hadn't been caught in their jimjams in the middle of the night. Pretending to clean windows. But really watching people snog.

The twins were ready for an action-packed day of being really odd. Dibdobs said in her beamy way, "Morning, Tallulah! Say morning, boys. To Tallulah."

They looked at me.

Sam said, "Oo been seeping?"

Dibdobs laughed, "Yes, clever boy, Tallulah has been sleeping and now she's awake and going to school. Hurrah!!!"

But I don't think Sam meant had I been sleeping. I think he meant had I been seeping. Because then he said, "I been seeping a lot."

Dobbs said, "Yes, clever boy, you've been sleeping too. Like Tallulah. You've been sleeping in your beddy-byes and now you are up and dressed!"

Max said, "No! Lady!!! He not seeped in his beddy-byes, he seeped in his pants!"

I had to go.

I met Vaisey by the post office. She had her hair in a plait so it didn't stick out.

She said, "Ruby plaited it for me. Do you think it looks all right?"

I said, "Yes, it looks nice."

I think she is wearing a bra, she seems more sticky-outy somehow. I didn't ask her, but I might sneak a look later on.

I do like her, she's so friendly. And she seems all excited and happy.

She said, "Did you do your assignment? What words did you come up with?"

Before I could tell her she went on. "At first I was think-ing about what people said about me, you know . . . nice. Bit young. Mad red hair, sticky-out bottom. But somehow, 'nice, young, red hair, big bum' didn't make me feel good. And then I thought the words that sum me up are 'Black Beauty.'"

I said, "Um, that's a horse."

As we walked through the woods she said, "*Black Beauty* was my all-time top favorite book when I was little."

I said, "Yes, but you didn't want to BE a horse, did you? You wanted to HAVE a horse."

Vaisey said, "No, I wanted to be the horse. I was Black Beauty."

"You were Black Beauty?"

"Yes, you know, free and galloping and so on. With black hair like yours. Not red hair. Sometimes just trotting along. Or cantering in high spirits. Look, I can even do dressage."

As we went up the lane to Dother Hall she started lift-ing one leg really high, and leaving it there for a second, and then hopping onto the other one and lifting that really high. And then crisscrossing her legs to the side.

She said, "I used to ride as Black Beauty to school."

She trotted the rest of the way to college. Occasionally when she veered off toward Woolfe Academy, I shouted, "Black Beauty, steady!"

★ ★ ★

I told her that when I went to school, I rode an imaginary Harley-Davidson motorbike.

As we reached the gates Vaisey reined herself in and said, "What words did you think of to describe you?"

And I said, "Um, it's a surprise."

And I wasn't fibbing because I haven't thought of anything.

When we arrived at the entrance hall other girls, older than us, were dashing in saying stuff like, "Hello, darling, I saw the BEST Beckett the other day. I wept it was soooo good," and "Hi hi, one and all. God, nobody can lend me any panstick, can they? I completely forgot mine this morning after London."

They must be the permanent students. I wonder if I will ever be like them.

Gudrun was there to greet us.

"Guten Tag, Fräulein!!! Wunderbar!!"

And she actually got hold of Vaisey's cheek and shook it between her fingers. She was still going, "Ooooooohhhh, look at you!"

I'm glad she didn't do it to me because I am easily startled.

Our little group gathered together feeling a bit shy and lost. Gudrun shepherded us into the main hall, her bun waving about wildly. She said, "Ms. Beaver wants you to go straight up on the stage, so that she can introduce you to the rest of the college."

We shuffled up and sat down on the chairs there. I looked out over the sea of faces. Were the faces looking at my knees? I had done my best to play the knees down by wearing black trousers. I curled my legs under the chair.

Everyone in the auditorium was chatting away, looking relaxed and cool. Vaisey looked at me and gave me a little thumbs-up. Then, from the side of the hall, Gudrun sounded a big gong and Sidone Beaver entered stage left. All of the girls stood up, so we did too.

Sidone wafted backward and forward. She was doing her world-renowned "filling the stage" thing.

Looking round, she smiled and then swept a hand across her body toward us.

"Girls of Dother Hall, I present fresh blood. I present to you these embryos. Will they grow into infants of theater, dance, music, art? Perhaps one or two of them will be giants of mime, or others medium-sized players of harps, others tiny but perfectly formed backstage scene shifters. It doesn't matter. What matters is the playing, the taking part in this wonderful adventure."

Sidone went on. "I want you to welcome our new little embryos into the bosoms of the Mother ship or Dother ship."

Sidone laughed in a tinkling way.

She said, "Did you see what I did there, girls?"

There was almost universal nodding from the audience.

Sidone said, "And to introduce themselves I have asked our new shipmates to come up with a word or words that sum them up. So now I ask you, new little friends, to tell us your words. And then, this is the bit you didn't know, I want you to improvise a movement or dance to go with the word or words."

What?

That hadn't been in our note.

We all looked at one another.

A dance?

Oh, Holy Mother of Mercy.

I hadn't even thought of any words! Perhaps I could just faint and that would be good. Then I'd be dragged offstage and taken. . . .

Sidone pointed to the end of the line.

"Let's start here. What is your outside name? Your pre–magic of theater name."

She was pointing at Jo.

Jo looked like an astonished (tiny) rabbit. She stood up.

You couldn't say she hadn't got pluck. You could say she was insane, but you couldn't say that she wasn't plucky. Anyway, she said, "My name is Jo."

Sidone beamed at her.

"Jo . . . Jooooooo . . . say it loud, Jooooooo."

Jo said it loud. "JOOOOOOOOOOO!!"

She's got a loud voice for a short person.

Sidone stepped away from her a little and then went on. "And what was your descriptive word or phrase, Jooooo?"

Jo said, "Well, it's 'strong.'"

Sidone said, "Good, good. Jo is strong. How would you show us that, Jo? That 'strong.' Show us your 'strong,' Jo. Show it! Use the whole space!!!"

And in front of our amazed gaze, Jo started growling.

Sidone encouraged her, "Good, good, I am feeling your strength."

Jo was feeling her strength as well. She started stomping around with her face all screwed up. And undoing her cardigan and puffing out her chest.

Vaisey whispered to me, "What is she doing?"

I said, "I think she's being the Hulk."

Vaisey was next. Alarm bells must have been ringing with Sidone because when Vaisey said "Black Beauty" she said quickly, "Now, Vaisey. We have just had a lot of charging energy from Jo and we need a change of pace. Perhaps you might like to think of prancing rather than galloping?"

Vaisey said, "I was going to do dressage."

Sidone said, "Excellent. Trot on."

And Vaisey did her leg holding and crisscrossing.

I could see some of the girls in the audience laughing.

Honey's dance was waggling her hips from side to side and going, "Mmmmmmmmmmmmm, yummy! Mmmm-mmmmmmmm, yummy."

Milly did "cheerful" (mostly very scary smiling), Becka

did "lighthearted" (skipping and clapping), and Tilly did "thoughtful" (frowning and skipping).

When it was Flossie's turn she said her word was "grand" in a Southern drawl and then started quietly going, "Oklahoma . . . Oklahoma . . . Oklahoma . . ."

Then she belted out, "The land we belong to is GRAND! And when I sayyyyyyyy . . . Hiyipppy yayyyyy . . . I'm saying you're doing fine, Oklahoma . . ." And doing big arm movements and high kicks.

She would have done the whole song if Ms. Beaver hadn't caught her firmly round the arms. Some people clapped at the end.

Then it was my turn. My brain had frozen over. In terror.

I stood up and my legs felt like jelly, with jelly knees. Sidone looked at me. "Well, Tallulah, what have you chosen?"

Yes, a very good point.

I looked out at the sea of faces. And I stood there. And then for some reason, I remembered my grandparents coming round to our house when I was little and in bed. After a few Guinnesses I would hear the Irish records being put on and then, "Get the bairn up and daaaancing!" And I would be got out of bed and put up on the table in the dining room to dance.

I started singing, *"Hiddly diddly diddly."* In an Irish accent. To an Irish tune that nobody has ever heard of,

62

because it doesn't exist. I started doing Irish dancing, keeping my arms straight by my sides and kicking my legs about whilst hopping on tippy-toes.

I don't know whether you have ever seen Irish dancing, but you've probably never seen it done by someone with eight-foot legs. I struck Sidone a glancing blow with my foot as I turned round.

I like to think it was a showstopper.

In the break we all went to the café to calm down.

Flossie, Vaisey, Jo, and I sat together. Shipwrecked from the Dother ship.

A group of older girls came over. The leader was a slim girl with copper-colored hair and very blue eyes, wearing expensive-looking clothes. She looked about seventeen or eighteen.

She said in a really false Irish accent, "Now would you be an Oirish colleen, to be sure, to be sure?"

She was talking to me.

I said, "Well, yes, half of my family is Irish, and the other—"

Before I could go on any further she said, in a very posh voice, "That was railly fun. Railly fun. Wasn't it, girls?"

The other two were nodding and looking. And saying, "Ya, raaillly fun. Well done."

The blue-eyed girl said, "You did railly, railly well. I'm Lavinia, and this is Dav and Anouska. Noos for short."

The others said, "Yeah, hi."

Lavinia went on. "You mustn't feel that you made berks of yourselves." And she looked directly at me when she said that bit.

Vaisey said, "Are you on the proper course?"

Lavinia laughed, "Yes, it can be hell, but I suppose we must love it! Come and see the performance lunchtime, some of us are doing a work in progress. See you later, begorrah, bejesus."

After they'd gone, Vaisey said, "She seems very nice, doesn't she? Good-looking too, isn't she?"

Flossie was chewing her hair. "Hmmmmm."

I said, "What does 'hmmmmm' mean?"

Flossie said, "She does seem nice, but I wanted to squeeze her head, and my head-squeezing instincts are usually good."

Out of control yoof

FOR THE REST OF THE MORNING Gudrun took us round for a tour of Dother Hall. We saw the studios for painting, the kiln area, the technical workshop. The backstage dressing rooms. We even went down to the music recording studios. Bob's office is to one side and Gudrun said, "We can just 'Bob' in."

He didn't hear us "Bob-ing," though, because he had heavy metal booming out of his speakers and he was pretending to play a guitar.

I said, "I didn't know that Mrs. Rochester was musical."

The others sniggered. Which was quite a nice feeling. After our tour, we were all lying down on the grass when Sidone came across to us. She was wearing an enormous hat and dark glasses.

"Darlings, darlings. Are you having fun? So, so thrilling, isn't it?"

We mumbled, "Yes."

She went on. "Now then, all in to the studio theater for the performance lunchtime. It's a work in progress by some of the seniors called 'Untitled . . . Now!' Oh, and by the way, girls, please use the upstairs loos for the rest of the day. There has been an unfortunate blockage situation which Bob is trying to get to the bottom of."

I didn't look at the others.

In the studio we were handed slips of paper.

Untitled . . . Now!

Question: What is a woman?
Is it a Woe . . . man?
Is it a Wombman?
How can we re-find our egg-sistence?
A work in progress by Lavinia Pilkington,
Davinia McCloud, and Anouska Pritchard
With thanks to the example of our
inspirational teacher Sidone Beaver

The studio went black and a faint spotlight came up in the center. Lavinia walked into it. She was carrying an apple. She walked right into the center of the light and looked at us meaningfully. She pointed to the apple and said, "Orange."

And smiled sadly.

Then Dav and Noos came on with scarves all over them and started snaking about chanting, "I saw the snake, I saw the snake, and the snake saw me."

Lav went off backward and walked back on a minute later, slowly carrying an egg.

The snakes were still giving it their all with the scarves. Lavinia said in a dramatic voice, "We come from eggs, but some of us are eggier than others."

She looked at the snakes, they looked back, and then they all smiled ironically.

They were still smiling ironically as the light went down very, very slowly.

Sidone started clapping so we joined in. I don't know why.

Gudrun, who was right at the front, was looking back at us and beaming like she had just seen an elephant reading a poetry book.

Afterward, Lav and Dav and Noos explained what it was about. Lav said, "I think what we were trying to get to is . . . you know, our sort of similar eggness. How women should stick together and support each other."

One of the snakes (Dav) said, "Yes, the bit where I come on and I'm still being the snake . . . but I am aware of the, of the . . ."

Lavinia said, "Of the egg?"

And Noos nodded enthusiastically.

"Yes, yes, yes, exactly."

Lavinia interrupted. "Yes, good point, Dav, and in fact one that I was just about to make . . . thanks for that. I wonder if anyone in the audience noticed that I became more egg-shaped during the performance?"

As we went out, I said to Flossie, "Did you notice that Lavinia got more egg-shaped during the performance?"

Flossie said, "No, but then, as Lav said . . . some of us are eggier than others."

The next day, Sidone announced that our performance project for the summer course is *Wuthering Heights*. The fifteen of us have to adapt and present an original reworking of it. Sidone said, "Go out and see what the countryside suggests to you."

Outside in the warm sunshine again, I began to cheer up. My new friends had been nice to me about the hiddly-diddly thing. In fact, Vaisey said, "It was unique."

And the others nodded.

Jo said, "It was almost in a way . . . so weird that you might be . . . well, known for your weirdness."

That's good, isn't it?

I felt smooth and purry, like a cat in a cream shop. With new friendies and no grown-ups to tell me off. I know that the Dobbinses are officially grown-ups, but their idea of telling you off is to only give you a small bit of cake.

So everything was looking up, apart from having no boys to look at yet. We had the afternoon off for sketching and ideas.

I said, "So, Woolfe Academy is somewhere over there. On the other side of the woods."

Flossie said, "Maybe we should go in the direction of the sign and see what it suggests to us."

Milly and Tilly and the rest of the others forged off down by the river, and our little group went in the vague direction of Woolfe Academy.

After two minutes of pretend looking at stuff we were out of sight of Dother Hall and found a comfy tree with soft grass underneath it.

I said, "This soft grass suggests 'softness' to me, but also at the same time 'lying-down-ness.'"

As we lay around the tree, Vaisey had obviously been thinking about Honey and her snogging stories. She said, "How did you get a boy to kiss you the first time? Did you say 'give us a kiss'?"

Honey lay down on her back and, putting her legs up against the tree, said, "Well, yeth, in a way. I did it with my eyeth. I did eyeth work."

Eyeth work?

Honey looks at boys she wants to snog. And they can tell from her eyes. She reckons that girls should be the ones who decide stuff.

Flossie said, "Well, that's all very well for you, you

smoothy smooth person, but I'm quite big. I think I frighten boys with my bigness."

I said, "And your violence."

Flossie said, "Granted."

Honey was still being the Love expert. She said, "If you think you are gorgeouth then boyth think tho too."

That was a novel idea.

Honey said, "You thtart off with thinking about your-thelf in all your glorwee."

I said, "I don't think I've got a glorwee."

Vaisey said, "She means in all your glory."

And she really did mean that. Not in all your glory with all your clothes on, but in all your glory in the er . . . in the *buenas noches señor*. In the pink pajamas. Or as the French say, *dans votre sans pantalons*.

She said that we had to love every bit of ourselves and stop criticizing our knees.

We should imagine we are in the *buenas noches señor* and feel free.

Jo said, "Like in that book where the boys all go native."

Honey said, "Yeth, thort of, but don't they eat each other in the end?"

Honey got up slowly. "Say, pwoudly . . . Oooooohhhh, I'm gorgeouth!"

We all sat there.

She said, "Do you want boyfwendth?"

We got up.

She started sidling up to the tree saying to it, "Ooohhh, I'm gorgeouth. I weally, weally am."

And she was shaking her bosoms at it and waggling her legs about.

She was so confident, it was amazing.

And sort of catching.

Vaisey started waggling her bottom at the tree saying, "Look at my lovely bottom, it's like a lovely . . . jelly!"

Flossie was shouting, "Why!! You're beeaauuutiful!!!"

It was very catching.

And I let rip with my legs.

As Jo was sweeping her hair up and down the tree, I was yelling at it, "You know you want the knees!!! Offer yourself to the knees!!!"

Then a voice behind us said, "Quickly, get a bucket of water, it's a girl fest!"

We all looked round and a shortish boy with a dark brown, floppy fringe and good-looking face was grinning at us. Behind him was another boy, taller, with wavy, dark blond hair. Also grinning.

None of us knew what to say. Perhaps we could pretend we were druids.

Jo eventually said, "Who are you, lurking about . . . er . . . lurking at people, who are . . ."

I said, ". . . who are doing a theatrical workshop."

The floppy-haired one was Phil and the blond one, Charlie. We told them our names and they leaned against the tree, looking at us. Phil has got a really nice smile, sort of twinkly, with nice teeth.

Then Charlie said to me, "Great kneework, Tallulah, if you don't mind me saying."

Crumbs.

Jo, who seemed to have developed the cocky gene suddenly, said to them, "What are you doing here?"

Phil said, "We are on a forced cross-country jog."

I said, "But you're not jogging."

Charlie said, "Well spotted."

Phil said, "We were on the jog, but we got tired of the jog."

Charlie went on, "We got tired of the jog just after we came out of the school gates. And thank goodness we did, otherwise we would have missed finding the 'Tree Sisters Club.'"

Phil said, "I would have never forgiven myself."

Vaisey said, "We are getting ideas for our *Wuthering Heights* performance."

We all nodded and I crossed my legs casually. Charlie smiled at me.

I said, "Yes, we are at the performing arts summer school at Dother Hall. That is what we are at. . . ."

I trailed off because both Phil and Charlie were looking at me.

Phil said, "So, let me get this right, you are all training to be lesbians?"

I said, "I think you mean thespians."

And Charlie said, "I know what I saw, love."

And he and Phil laughed.

And funnily enough, we all laughed. It must have looked bloody weird dancing round a tree and trying to get off with it.

We all relaxed then. It was exciting having two captive, real-life boys to talk to. Vaisey asked them about their school, Woolfe Academy. "What do you do there?"

Charlie said, "We get bored and depressed, mostly."

Phil said, "We're there because . . . well it's a small thing, really, there was a bit of . . . an incident at our, er, 'normal' school."

We looked at him.

Phil went on, "You know how it is with boys and homemade fireworks. And science labs that, you know . . . go . . ."

I said, "Go?"

Charlie said, "Up."

Phil went on, "So the bottom line is that we are at Woolfe Academy to be taught how to become decent citizens."

Wow.

Flossie said, "Are you, like, 'out of control yoof'?"

Phil said, "Very like that."

Vaisey said, "Is it because your parents don't understand you?"

Charlie said, "No, it's because our parents understand us very well, and that is why they wanted us to go away."

Phil was nodding wisely. "Yes, we are here to learn how to become normal young men, and to do that we have to jog everywhere with rucksacks on our backs. That is the key."

Charlie went on, "Although, to be frank, if the headmaster had his way we would be hopping everywhere. Just to show us what real life is really about. He's only got one leg."

Out of the blue, Phil said to Jo, "I liked your hair dance thing. Was that the magic of modern dance?"

Jo frowned. And jabbered on like Jabber the Wok. "Yes. We do dance at college, in fact, hahahahaha, Tallulah has already done Irish dancing. She kneed the headmistress. Onstage. In front of everyone."

Oh, thank you very much, new, strong, but thickish friend.

Charlie said, "Wow! You kneed the headmistress. Would you mind if I touched the sacred knees?"

What did that mean?

Was he joking?

Or had my knees made a real impact?

At that moment, there was a piercing whistle and the sound of pounding feet in the near distance. A voice yelled, "OK, lads, keep it up! Well run, Miles Senior, just the plowed field, through the copse and home. Keep it up!!"

Phil and Charlie got up and started jogging on the spot.

Phil said, "Time to take our surprise lead at the other end of the copse."

As they jogged off, Charlie shouted, "Ta-ta, don't be strangers!"

And they were gone.

Wow.

And phew.

He had everything a dream boy should have

AMBLING TO THE VILLAGE on Thursday with Jo and Flossie and Vaisey—Honey has a singing lesson so she is off to the music studio—we were, of course, talking about the boys. Phil and Charlie.

Vaisey said, "I thought they were both quite cute. And friendly. And funny. How can we see them again? Should we go and hang around the tree every day?"

Jo said, "Phil was cute, wasn't he? But he's a bit short."

I said, "Jo, you know that saying 'It's like the pot calling the kettle black'? Well, you saying that Phil is a bit short, is like a tiny, tiny, black pot calling a tiny kettle black."

When we reached Heckmondwhite, Flossie and Jo went into the village shop to get emergency supplies to stave off

76

night starvation. Fun-sized Mars bars mainly. And Vaisey and I did hanging-about duties.

As we lolled on the wall, Ruby came out of The Blind Pig. I hadn't seen her since Sunday and it was nice to see her little face.

She called out, "Nah then!"

What did that mean?

Ruby asked us what we had been doing at college.

I told her, "In a nutshell, I did some Irish knee dancing, Vaisey trotted about pretending to be Black Beauty . . . and then we met some boys from Woolfe Academy, lurking in the undergrowth."

Ruby said, "Why were you lurking in the undergrowth?"

Vaisey said, "Not us, them. Boys. They were quite cute, weren't they, Lullah? But . . . anyway, you are too young for this sort of talk, Ruby. Did you play skipping and stuff today?"

Ruby just looked at her. "I've kissed boys, tha knows."

What?

She said, "There's nowt to it. It's natural, like cows and that."

Do cows kiss? I didn't know anything about anything.

Vaisey was amazed. "You've kissed boys?"

Ruby went on, "They allus want to kiss you. You have to shape them up a bit, some of them don't even know to take their chewing gum out."

I couldn't think of one single thing to say.

The others came out with their provisions and Ruby said, "I've found some owl eggs, do you want to see them?"

Jo and Flossie said they had to go, because they had a lot of provisions to get through, and Vaisey wanted to go and read *Wuthering Heights*. We have Dr. Lightowler tomorrow. Oh good. Or goooooooood as she might say. But probably not to me.

Vaisey toddled off.

I really like her.

And Rubes?

She's . . . well, what would you call her? Too little for a proper friend. A friendster? A mini friendster? A fun-sized friend?

She and I went down the side path that ran along the back of the Dobbinses' house. We bobbed down because I could see Dibdobs in the kitchen and I didn't want to have the staring brothers following us. As we passed my bedroom window at the back, I looked up to see what you could see. Quite a lot is what you could see. For instance, if someone had been, say, standing in the window in their pajamas, spying on you snogging. You could have seen that.

I said casually to Ruby, "Um, do you know a boy called . . . Cain?"

Ruby laughed. "Who doesn't know Cain? Who doesn't know the Hinchcliffs? Ruben and Seth are bad enough, but Cain . . ."

Oh, this was worse than I thought.

I said nervously, "What is this Cain . . . um . . . what does he, why is he, um . . ."

Ruby said, "He's all right really, but he's as much use as a chocolate teapot. The girls go mad for him, though. He's good-looking, I'll say that fer him, but the way he . . . well."

I couldn't help myself. "The way he . . . what?"

"Well, he goes out wi' girls and snogs 'em and then he dumps 'em. And gets another one, and then he goes back t'first and gets 'er again and then dumps 'er again. The amount of crying about that lad."

I said, "Well . . . I mean, more fool the girls for going out with him."

Ruby said, "Oh, he nivver takes 'em out anywhere. They just turn up to see his gigs."

I said, "What do you mean, 'they just turn up to see his gigs'?"

Ruby sighed, "The Hinchcliff boys formed a band called The Jones. They're right boring, they just moan on about stuff."

I said, "Like what?"

Ruby crinkled her nose up. "You know, stuff like . . . 'Girlfriend in the River, I Know, I Know It's Really

Serious' is one of their tunes. They've got one that Cain wrote about his girlfriend at the time. It's called 'Shut Up, Mardy Bum.'"

We'd reached an old barn and Ruby stopped her tale of Cain the Cad to say, "The eggs are in here at the far end. I'll just make sure Connie's not around or she'll attack our heads."

Connie? Attack our heads?

I said, "Does Connie own the barn?"

Ruby said, "No, you barm pot, Connie's the big mother owl."

Now I remembered Connie, snoozing as she ate the mouse.

I pulled my hat down.

We went farther into the dark barn and over to some hay bales. And there they were, the eggs, two of them. Glowing sort of whitely. We looked at them for a bit. It's quite fascinating, but, um, boring. I said, "When will they, you know, come out?"

She said, "Dust tha mean hatch?"

I nodded.

She said, "Abaht three to four weeks, I reckon."

We looked at them again.

Ruby said, "They're nice eggs, aren't they?"

I said to Ruby, "Ruby, do you think that we all have egginess in common?"

She looked at me. "Dad said this would happen. He said that you were all barmy and that if I hung around with you it would only be a matter of time before I was prancing around like a tit."

I said, "It's not me. This posh girl called Lavinia did an eggy performance. She said that she became more egg-shaped as she did it. I only did my accidental comedy version of Irish dancing."

Ruby said, "Go on then, do it for me."

I said, "I feel a bit shy."

Ruby just looked at me. "That'll be a help when you're on't stage in front of folk."

I said, "All right, I will . . . I'll do it, I'll just get in the mood by doing the intro music first."

Ruby sat on a hay bale and I got up on another one.

I started singing, "Well, hiddly diddly diddly dee. We're all off to Dublin in the green, in the green, hiddly diddly diddle dee . . ." And went into my dance. Arms by the side and leaping, leaping, leap. High kick, high kick, twirly ankle, twirly ankle.

Ruby was laughing like a drain when I heard the barn door creak open and a deep voice said, "Ruby, are you in here?"

Cain!

I tried to get behind the hay bale and promptly fell over it. Nearly smashing the owl eggs as well. As I was lying in the hay, the best-looking boy I have ever seen loomed over me. He was tall and long-limbed with a cool Fred Perry shirt on. I could see he had longish, thick hair and a lovely broad mouth. He smiled at me and held out a hand to pull me up.

"Hello, I'm Alex, Ruby's brother."

I said, "Hello, I'm . . . um . . ."

And I'd forgotten my own name.

Ruby seemed unfazed by this. She said, "She's called Tallulah and she goes to that bonkers school."

Alex laughed. "Rubes thinks that anyone who prats around on stage is mad."

I said, "Heehee, your dad said me and my friends were breeding."

Were you supposed to say "breeding" in front of best-looking boys?

To cover it up I said, "I nearly smashed up the owl eggs, but I didn't and I'm glad because we . . . we're all like eggs . . . in a way."

Ruby said, "Dunt start that bloody egg business agin."

It turns out that Alex is going to go to performing arts college in Liverpool! As we walked back from the barn I said, "Wow . . . um . . . oh, wow. Liverpool. That's, well, that's not . . . here, is it?"

He laughed again. "Nope."

He was sooooo lovely. And, well, gorgeous. He had everything a dream boy should have. Back, front, sides.

Everything. A head. And all in a boy shape.

When we got to the Dobbinses' gate, I said, *"Buenas noches!"* and giggled like a nitwit.

Ruby looked at me and rolled her eyes and then said, "I'm off."

As Ruby ran on home, Alex said, "Well, nice to meet you. Yeah, actually I'm coming up to the college sometime soon, doing some work with Monty."

I said, "Monty?"

"Monty de Courcy."

I said, "Oh, that Monty . . . hmm."

I nodded.

He said, "Nice to meet you, Tallulah. That must be one of the coolest names. Bye."

In my squirrel room.

I have met a dream boy, in boy form. He said I had a cool name.

He said nothing against my knees.

He couldn't actually see my knees, but . . .

I realize that in one day I've had more boy fun than I have had in fourteen and a half years. Today has made the bottom-touching kitbag incident fade into insignificance.

I LOVE Yorkshire. I do. I really do.

I'm not an Irish dancing broom

I CANNOT BELIEVE THAT Ruby has got such a gorgeous brother.

Alex.

Hmmmmmmmmmmmmmmmm.

I thought, I can hardly believe that a whole week has gone by.

A whole week since I first came to Dother Hall and nearly a whole day since I've seen Alex.

I have decided to wear my green top and tight zip-sided jeans. And a little cardi. And the flip-flops that Dad brought me back from Brazil. They are gold.

My hair is bouncy today. Should I backcomb the top bit to give it more umph?

As I looked in the bathroom mirror, the sun shone and beamed into my eyes. They gave me a bit of a turn. They do look very green indeed today. Funny to look at your own eyes and think, crumbs, that's a bit green.

Hey and hang on a minute, I think, maybe, when I look closely I can see little tiny bumps under my T-shirt. Woo-hoo! At this rate I might even be able to buy a bra by the time I am forty. Just in time for my pension.

Still, it's a start.

Two starts actually.

I went downstairs to the kitchen to find Dibdobs in ginormous shorts and a cowboy hat with bits of rope on it.

She looked up and gave me a salute. "Dib dib dib, Tallulah."

She put two boiled eggs on the table for me. They had little bobble hat things to keep them warm. Still, as I now know, we are all eggs deep down. Did that make it cannibalism if I ate them?

I removed an egg hat to smash its head in and Dibdobs said, "Harold made the egg hats. I did tell you we're going away this weekend. It's the Brownies camp for me and the boys. It's the tiddlywinks grand final, so it's all tension."

I started to say, "I haven't got my tiddles, um, or is it winks, so I couldn't possibly—"

She was smiling. "And Harold is going into the woods with his Iron Man group."

His what?

I said, "Well that sounds . . . wizard."

Dibdobs came and gave me a big hug. "I thought you would like to be with Vaisey, so I've arranged for you to stay at The Blind Pig—pop round there after college tonight."

I was doing secret inward sniggering. And a secret inward voice in my head was saying (in a strange breathy voice . . .), Yes, yessss, I will pop round to The Blind Pig. I will "pop" round because guess who lives at The Blind Pig? It is not a blind pig, it is Alex. Alex, the best-looking boy in the universe. Alex, who said I had a cool name. Alex, who . . .

And that is when the twins came in, both in huge shorts.

They came and stood an inch away from me to do their silent looking.

But I was too happy to be freaked out by them.

So I smiled at them in between mouthfuls of eggy.

They did what they think is smiling back.

The wobbly teefs have gone, so now when they smile it's like looking at sock creatures. If you can imagine that.

I left the house a bit earlier than I needed to, so that I could get to the pub and maybe accidentally-on-purpose bump into Alex. But Vaisey was already sitting on the wall waiting for me. Just as well, really, I would have probably said something insane and fallen over a leaf if I'd seen him.

And to be honest, he only said I had a cool name.

We mooched to Dother Hall and as it loomed into view I remembered that we had Dr. Lightowler for two hours. The roof still had its bit of old blanket flapping about. Mrs. Rochester is not a highly skilled worker. I hope for the girls' sakes it doesn't rain anytime soon.

After registration we crowded into the studio for Bob's "talk" on music and music technology.

I couldn't help noticing that his ponytail, burnt off in the dorm inferno, seems to have grown back. Twice the length.

I whispered to Flossie, "He's wearing a false ponytail."

Bob gave us the benefit of his many years "on the road" with bands.

"Listen up, dudes. Yes, I've toured with some of the greats. The legends. I've done all the big gigs: Wembo, Glasto."

Glasto? Wembo?

Bob looked at us.

"The Glastonbury."

Vaisey said, "Which bands did you do?"

Bob was twiddling with knobs and put his feet on the mixing desk. He was wearing leather Cuban- heeled boots. He put on his shades.

"The lot, the big boys—Floyd, Purple, Zep, Heap."

We looked at him. Who were Zep Heap? Or did he mean Purple Zep?

He let us bang a drum and rattle some maracas. It was

exciting when he showed us the sound booths and asked if anyone wanted a go. Vaisey and Jo sang a bit from *Grease* and Flossie and Honey did "Oo-oo-oooos" in the background.

"You're the one that I want . . ."

"Oo-oo-oooo."

They were good, actually.

Jo had to stand on a little box to reach the mike and Vaisey was moving her bottom around in time to the music.

Bob recorded it and then he did "multitracking" so it sounded like fourteen people singing. This is more like it.

I said to the girls, "I feel like part of this great big crazy world of showbiz, now!"

Bob said as we left, "The Jones are coming in to lay down a few tracks. It's not my sort of stuff, not heavy, just more indie landfill, but they're local so . . . you might want to come on down, chill out, and get your ears on."

Get our ears on?

I said, "Did he say 'chill out'? It doesn't seem right coming from a man with a false ponytail."

Anyway, I will not be going to see The Jones for love or money. In fact, if it is at all possible, I will never see any of the Hinchcliffs again.

Cain in particular.

We walked along to the small theater space for the dreaded Dr. Lightowler experience.

Dr. Lightowler swished in in her cloak. I wonder if she has a summer cloak and a winter cloak?

As part of the background for our end-of-summer-school performance of *Wuthering Heights*, Cloakwoman was telling us about the appalling life of the Brontës.

She said, "It's hard for you spoiled modern girls to imagine the evenings in that forsaken place, Haworth Vicarage . . . cooped up, imprisoned by the forces of nature, no escape, because of the weather, but also because they were women."

Dr. Lightowler was going on and on, swishing her cloak about as she talked. I wonder if she goes to bed in it?

"Now, girls, get up and start moving about in the space. Imagine that you are the Brontës. It's a dark winter afternoon. . . ." She snapped off all the lights and said, "I've got some torches here, girls, some of you come and take one and shine them in an improvised way."

She put on a torch in the dark and handed more to Honey and Vaisey and some others I couldn't see. She held a torch under her chin so it lit her up really weirdly.

She said in a spooky, guttural voice, "The light is gone by three, and the wind howls around the drafty cold house, making the candles gutter and cast strange shadowy shapes on the wall. Could some of you howl a bit?"

We howled like mad and she had to shout over the top of us.

"Girls, just light howling, please."

I said, "Okeydokey, Dr. Light-howler."

Which Vaisey thought was funny, but fortunately the doctor didn't hear.

We toned the howling down.

Dr. Lightowler went on. "Flossie, perhaps you are Emily huddling by the fire and trying to entertain your sisters. To take their minds off their bodies racked with consumption."

Two of the girls formed a fire with their torches, and Flossie huddled by it, shivering and coughing. She said in a Texan drawl, "Now y'all girls, come here a cotton-pickin' moment."

Dr. Lightowler said, "Emily is from Yorkshire, Flossie."

Flossie tried again. "Ay up, lasses, come around t'fire and we'll sing a song."

Dr. Lightowler came forward. "Milly, Tilly, be Anne and Charlotte."

Milly and Tilly came and huddled alongside Flossie, warming their hands at the torch fire.

Dr. Lightowler said to us in a hushed voice, "Perhaps they might make up little stories about the shadows? The rest of you girls be imaginary shapes guttering across the room. Girls with the torches, flicker them everywhere."

Be an imaginary shape?

Honey and the rest started swooping and fluttering about.

Tilly cried, "Oh, Emily, Charlotte, what is that? Over there by the fire extinguisher . . . um, by the . . . loom. . . . Why, is that an eagle? Er . . . hunting?"

And Flossie said, "Nay, lass, I think it's a witch, high on a broomstick."

I tried to join in, but I just felt like a twerp. Especially as when I did attempt to flutter about I caught myself in the midriff with the fire extinguisher. It crashed to the floor and Dr. Lightowler gave me a foul look. I tried to get it to stand up again, but it was making a hell of a noise clanking about.

The "Brontës" were excitedly saying, "I think I can see, I can hear . . . a little hand tapping at the window, is it Cathy out on the moors looking for Heathcliff????"

Then Flossie said, "Yes, yes, I can hear it, what is that over there?"

And she pointed at me. And everyone stopped and shone their torches on me.

So I put my arms down by my side and bobbed about.

I don't know why I do Riverdance when I'm in the spotlight. I must have an inner Irish dancer trying to get out.

Everyone started laughing.

Apart from Dr. Lightowler, who said, "What are you doing, Tallulah Casey?"

I said, "Um, I'm sweeping up. I'm an Irish broomstick."

I could see Flossie put her fist into her mouth and Jo had a coughing fit.

Dr. Lightowler just looked at me.

I can see that inwardly she's ticking me off her list of people for next year's places.

Do you think my corkers are growing?

As WE WALKED DOWN the long main corridor toward the café, Vaisey said, "Ruby was telling me about The Jones. They are supposed to be cool, but moody. And the lead singer is called Cain, that's la gothic, isn't it?"

Cain.

I didn't answer. Where to begin? Where to end?

The Mark of Cain.

I am haunted by Cain.

And now he could be somewhere in the building.

I would wear my hat and pull it right down.

I put it on in the loos. Avoiding looking at Bob's notice about my smalls, which makes me feel somehow dirty.

When I came out Lavinia and her mates were coming out of the dance studios wearing ballet shoes and leggings.

Lav was saying to Dav, "I love the ballet, just love it. If I was as slim as you, Dav, I would go for it like a shot."

Dav said, "But Lav, you've got a railly, railly nice figure and anyway you are soooo good at modern and jazz. Madame Frances said she had never seen better jazz hands."

Lavinia said, "Now you are just being a railly big love."

When she saw us, Lavinia gave me a number fifty-eight on the beam-o-meter. Really beaming. Like she really liked me. Perhaps she did.

She twitched my hat, which is annoying. Especially as it had probably made my hair stick up. She said, "Sweet. How you doing, little Oirish, are you oiright?"

Then Lavinia said, "Oh, and there is another performance lunchtime in a fortnight, you should try and do a little something for it. I'd be glad to help with anything you have an idea about."

And she went bouncing off. She is very bouncy, if you know what I mean.

Vaisey said, "She's really nice, isn't she?"

Flossie said, "Hmm."

And I said, "Hmm."

But not in an entirely good "hmm" way.

It was a lovely day and Jo said, "Oh, I don't know. Where should we have lunch—here, do you think? Or it's such a nice day . . . what about in the woods, maybe?"

And we all went, "Oh . . . yeah, that's a good idea. If you like, yeah. I don't mind." Really casually. As if we hadn't given meeting Charlie and Phil a second thought.

We went into the woods and settled down under the dancing tree.

Talking about our morning, I said, "Dr. Lightowler hates me."

Vaisey said, "You're not wrong. But why did you have to be a broom? Why couldn't you just flit around being a bat? Anything. Why a dancing Irish broomstick?"

I said, "I don't know, it's because she notices me so much, it makes my brain freeze and when my brain freezes my legs get out of control."

Jo was munching her way through twenty-five apples. She's got a very healthy appetite for a small person. She said, "I wonder if the Woolfe boys will come over. Have you seen them around the village?"

I said, "Why, are you missing them?"

Jo nearly choked on her Granny Smith. "No. How could I miss them when I don't know them?"

Flossie said, "I think you've been thinking about Phil, haven't you? You were talking in your sleep last night saying, 'Phil, Phil, I want you.'"

Jo said, "I was not. Anyway, how would you know? I had to come and put your teddy pajama case over your face to drown out your snoring."

Flossie said, "Are you telling me that you touched my

teddy pajama case in the night?"

Jo said, "Yes."

Flossie got up. "That does it. Come on, let's fight. You teddy toucher."

Jo got up and said, "I warn you, I'm smallish, but . . ."

Flossie, who was limbering up like a prizefighter, said, "I know, I know, I've seen your inner Hulk. Come on!! I've been cramped up in that damn vicarage all morning with consumption. I want to live, I want to live!!!!!"

I got up then and shouted, "I am not an Irish dancing broomstick, I'm a human being!!!!"

And suddenly it turned into a wrestling match. Even Honey tucked her skirt into her knickers and dived onto the top of the pile.

I couldn't see my feet.

But I knew what I could feel.

I said, "Oy, will whoever is grasping my nearly corker area get off."

I heard Vaisey's muffled voice say, "Sorry, I was just stopping myself from falling over."

Then Flossie, who had my head in an armlock, said, "Oy, leave my bum alone!"

And that is when a lad's voice joined in. "Bloody hell, fightin' lasses!"

What!

When we eventually disentangled and got up, in front of us were two very dark-haired boys. Is there a whole tribe of forest boys who just appear all the time when girls are doing private group work? They had leather jackets on and slung around their necks were guitars in guitar cases. I recognized them. Oh goodie. They were the two boys I had seen fighting on the bench on my second day in Heckmondwhite. I took a bit of a twig that had got caught in my leggings and put it in my mouth like a cigarette. I don't know why.

There was something menacing about the boys. They were staring at us from under their dark hair.

"C'mon, Seth, we've got no time for silly lasses."

Seth?

Not Seth Hinchcliff.

They started bowling off toward Dother Hall.

Then the one called Seth turned round and stopped. He looked at Flossie, who was just getting to her feet and smoothing down her skirt.

She looked him straight in the eye and he said, "Tha's not bad. I wouldn't mind laiking about with thee."

And he turned and went off.

Even Flossie was speechless.

Who did they think they were?!!

We soon found out who they thought they were when we got back to Dother Hall, because there was a big group of girls hanging about the studio in the corridor.

Milly and Tilly spoke at the same time. Breathlessly. "Have you seen them?"

Becka said, "The Jones. They're here."

★ ★ ★

We went along to the dance studio for our first dance class with Madame Frances. She had been classically trained and, as she said herself, "I danced with all the greats, in the chorus at first, of course, but just as I was chosen to dance the Swan I suffered my"—and here she hesitated and her voice went quiet and husky—"injury."

She was silent for so long that eventually, just to be polite, I said, "What, um, did you injure, Madame?"

She looked up and said, "No, no, you young things don't need to know about me. I don't complain. I soldier on. Would one of you just go to my drawer and fetch me my wrap? I feel strangely chilled."

Someone sloped off to the drawer and got her wrap. Then her thermos flask. Then a little stool to rest her foot on. Then her stick, which she had left at the far end of the studio.

Eventually she said, "Now, girls, all to one end of the studio and let's begin and have a little warm-up. Could someone get my drum . . . ?"

And that was it, that was our first dance workshop. For about an hour, Madame Frances sat on her chair in her wrap drinking tea from her thermos flask with one hand and hitting a drum with her stick. And we had to run across the room. In time to the drum. Backward, forward, sideways. Spinning, leaping, running, you name it, we did it to the drum.

It was exhausting.

Madame Frances might not be able to stand up but she could certainly bang a drum.

My hair was all over the place and Vaisey looked like she'd been thrown in a vat of tomatoes. So we nipped to the loos and chucked water over our heads (not even saving it to do our smalls).

When we came down again at break there was a huge gaggle of girls trying to see into the music studios. Good, that meant that The Jones wouldn't be able to get out very easily.

At this point there was a big kerfuffle. Girls were sort of semifainting. Then we heard a voice I recognized saying, "Stop being so nebby, you lasses, and get your apple catchers out of t'road. Afore I do it for thee."

It was Ruben. The Jones came out of the studio looking a bit moody.

I got my hat and pulled it right down over my eyes so that Cain wouldn't recognize me.

But when I peeped out there was no sign of Cain.

Flossie said, "Have you finished recording already?"

The other one, not Ruben so it must be Seth, looked like he was going to kill her.

"No, we haven't finished recording. Bloody Cain niv-ver showed up."

As they went through the front doors, pursued by girls,

Ruben said, "I don't know why we let him be in the band, he can't sing and he's an idle git."

Seth said, "I tell you why we let 'im be in the band: the lasses come to see 'im, 'e writes the lyrics, and 'e's our brother."

On the way home Vaisey said, "Honey's quite, you know . . . advanced for her age, isn't she? She told me she's a size thirty-four C."

I looked at Vaisey sideways and said casually, "Yeah, yeah, she would be about that. What are you . . . about a thirty-two, um . . . ?"

Vaisey looked down at herself.

"Yeah, I'm thirty-two B. So far."

I looked down at myself and she looked as well.

We walked on in silence for a bit.

Then I said, "Do you think my corkers are growing?"

Vaisey looked closer and said, "Yes, I think they are. Maybe you could do some exercises. Like press-ups."

Hmmm.

I said, "Oh yes. I could do the massage and press-ups combined."

Vaisey said, "Massage?"

I didn't mention the corker-rubbing business because there is something about Vaisey that makes me think she would find it unhygienic. And also we were sharing a bed tonight. Sharing a bed with Vaisey, but sharing a pub with Alex.

When we got to Heckmondwhite I said I would see her in about an hour and scampered to the Dobbinses'. I unlocked the door. Aaaah, the peace and tranquillity. No looming mad twins, no huge shorts. I walked around the kitchen just for the sheer pleasure of not having anyone staring at me from the floor.

In my squirrel room, I opened the window. It was still quite hot. I was putting together my little overnight bag when I thought, what if I unexpectedly bump into Alex on my way to the lala in the middle of the night? What should I say?

What about a quirky saying? To enhance my quirky nature.

What about, "Cor, love a duck, I didn't see you there, young sir!"

No no no!!!

I didn't want him to see me in my jimjams.

And what about if he said, "Do you fancy a ride in my car?"

What is good car wear?

A hat?

For wind?

Or a headscarf?

I haven't got a headscarf.

Well that's it then, isn't it? The whole thing is ruined. I haven't even got a headscarf to go out in his car.

I can't think about this.

I'm going to do deep breathing.

I looked out my window across the fields, toward Grimbottom.

Me and the girls are going to go to Skipley tomorrow. On the bus! Who would have thought I would be so excited about going on a bus. But there might be civilization in Skipley. There might be a Topshop. I am soooo excited. I am overexcited. I'm hysterical, I may have to slap my own face in a minute at this rate.

I got my things and left the house quickly. As I crossed the village green, I saw that Alex was outside The Blind Pig sitting on the wall. I got the funny thumpy-heart thing. I must think of something sensible to say ahead of time.

What would be normal to talk about?

He smiled when he saw me.

Ooooohhh, he was smiling. He was doing the smiling thing. Oooooooh.

"Ay up, Tallulah, are you all right?"

I smiled back and kept my jacket done up to de-emphasize my lack of corkers.

Alex was sitting with his legs crossed and his hands in his pockets. The sun was still quite bright and he screwed his eyes up so that he could see me. He looked lovely with screwy-up eyes.

He said, "What are you up to tonight, then?"

I said in an offhand way, "I'm staying at yours, actually,

because Dibdobs has gone off making acorn pies with the Brownies."

He laughed.

And then I couldn't think of anything else to say.

He said, "What have you been up to at college?"

I said, "Well, we did an improvised thingy about the Brontës. You know, howling winds . . . woooooooo. And then we did leaping and there's going to be a performance lunchtime about, um . . . well, I thought I might do the owl eggs."

He looked puzzled.

"Eggs?"

Oh noooo. Now I had started an egg thing. Again. Because I had been thinking about the last time I saw him in the barn. I couldn't back out of it, so I said, "Yeah, you know, the, well, I was thinking about the owl eggs and I thought I might do a performance about them."

He still looked at me and didn't say anything.

So I went on. "Yeah, because Ruby told me that when they are born, the owl twins will have double eyelids, which is, um . . . interesting."

And I started doing an impression of double eyelids for him.

Not that he had asked me.

But as I had started I couldn't stop. I raised my bottom eyelids really slowly upward without moving my upper eyelids. Which is hard, actually.

Alex folded his arms and leaned back and said, "How old are you?"

And I said, "Hahahahaha, old enough."

Why? Old enough for what? To be friends with eggs?

Just then a car drew up with a boy driving and honked its horn. Alex slid off the wall and waved at the bloke. Then he said to me, "Have fun. Don't lead my sister into bad ways."

And he went off and got in the car.

Ruby came out with Matilda, her bulldog, and waved Matilda's paw at him. And the car drove off.

I said, as casually as I could, "So where is, um . . . Alex off to?"

She looked at me and said, "Don't even think about it."

I daren't ask Ruby anything else about Alex. I felt a bit sad. And stupid at the same time.

But it was good fun with Vaisey and Ruby. We had our tea in the pub kitchen served by Mr. Barraclough, Ruby's dad. I'd never seen Ruby's mum and I didn't like to ask where she was.

Mr. Barraclough said, "What will you artists be up to tonight, then? Will you be pretending to be stuck in an imaginary cupboard?"

Ruby said, "Dad, can we have crisps?"

He said, "Yes, just as long as you don't let these two make them into anything unusual."

And he went laughing off into the bar.

He's big. He ate fifteen pies at the pie-eating contest.

So we just messed about upstairs in the pub. Vaisey and me worked out what we were going to wear to go to Skipley and tried out different makeup. Vaisey is quite good with makeup. She drew a dark brown pencil line around my eyes and I thought it made me look a bit more grown-up. Sort of more moody and less startled.

Vaisey said, "You should wear a darker pink lipstick."

I said, "How do you know that sort of thing?"

And she showed me some mags that she had, that told you all sorts of stuff. In the makeup and hair guide it said you should wear makeup to balance your shape. And then there were pictures of girls with a square face, and a round face, and a long face; one with big lips and one with thin lips; narrow forehead, chubby cheeks, no cheeks. It was a nightmare trying to choose what I had. In the end we sort of agreed I was a longy roundy biggy-faced person.

Which is a help.

I said to Vaisey, "It's all right for you, you're that one in the middle."

Vaisey said, "The turned-up nose, sticky-out hair, small-cheeked, round-faced person?"

I said, "Exactly."

Then I said, "You're cute as a button, though."

She smiled at me.

She is cute as a button.

We let Ruby use our lipsticks and eye shadows and I said I will get her something tomorrow from town. Her dad shouted up the stairs, "Oy, Ruby, beddy-byes for thee."

She went off to her bedroom.

Vaisey and I were sleeping in the same bed. It was cozy because we could hear the sounds from the pub downstairs. A lot of laughing and singing.

The bedroom door creaked open and Ruby came in in her nightie with Matilda. She and Matilda looked at us. Matilda is not what you would call athletic. Well, what you could call her is a really odd-looking barrel thing with short, stubby legs. But she is the friendliest doggy in the world and loves everyone.

Ruby said, "Matilda wanted to see you."

And then Matilda threw herself at the bed. She meant to come up on the bed with us, but she is too short, so she just kept hurling herself at it and bouncing off the side. Sometimes she would manage to get her front legs on the bed before she slowly toppled off. It was very funny.

Ruby got into the bottom of the bed and tucked herself in.

She said, "Come on, Matilda, upsy daisy."

Which was a bit mean as it was never going to happen unless someone brought a ladder.

In the end we hauled her up and into bed with us. It

made us laugh a lot seeing her tucked up under the sheets.

Especially when Ruby went and got Matilda's special Noddy sleeping hat.

The volume downstairs in the pub got louder, as did the singing.

I said, "What is that song they are singing? Is it an old Yorkshire ditty, you know, like that 'On Ilkley Moor Bar T'at'?"

Ruby said, "Nah, it's a football song. It goes 'We hate Chelsea, we hate Chelsea, we are the Chelsea haters.'"

Lying in my squirrel room

WHEN WE WOKE UP on Saturday morning I had been sleeping on my face. Partly because I woke up in the middle of the night thinking that I was having a heart attack. My chest was all heavy and I couldn't breathe properly. Then I realized that Matilda was sleeping on it. So I pushed her onto the back of my legs and slept the other way round.

It was not the best night's sleep I've ever had, because I had Ruby's foot practically up my bottom as well. But it was sort of cozy.

When I went to the bathroom and looked in the mirror, it was like Matilda staring back at me because my face was all squashy and flattened.

Vaisey said, "Put hot flannels on it and sort of smooth it out."

She is a mine of beauty tips.

★ ★ ★

We were meeting Jo and Flossie this morning at eleven o'clock at the bus stop.

Vaisey was "modeling" things that she might wear. It was a lovely day, no sign of imminent fog, so she was going for a "summer girl" look.

She's got lots of nice dresses. I don't really know about dresses, I am so busy trying to disguise my legs and knees.

I said to Vaisey, "I wish I could wear stuff like you do."

She was trying on a little denim dress and said, "You will, your legs are bound to stop growing soon."

In the end I put my jeans on, but I did borrow a studded leather belt from Vaisey which looked good, I think. Vaisey did my eyeliner thing and I wore a bit of dark pink lip gloss.

Flossie and Jo were at the stop when we got there. They'd got out onto the roof last night and were really excited about it.

Jo said, "It was brilliant, we danced around in our pajamas and no one knew we were up there!"

Flossie said, "We could have stayed up there all night and they wouldn't have known."

Jo said, "I'd kept some bread and butter back from supper and we ate that. Outdoors. On the roof."

I said, "We had a bulldog in our bed."

Flossie said, "You lucky, lucky person. You have all the luck."

* * *

The bus for Skipley arrived. It was quite full. When I asked for four returns to Skipley, please, the bus driver said, "You'll not come back from Skipley, lass, no one does. You're all doomed!!!! Especially since I will be driving today with no hands."

Then he started laughing and put his hands behind his back.

A woman at the front said, "Take no notice, love, he amuses himself."

Then a grumpy voice from the back said, "What's the bloody holdup? Ay, aren't you that gangly one that kicked me on the train? I'm eighty-five, you know. By the time you bloody lot get on, I'll be nearer eighty-six."

We sat very near the front.

And everyone looked at me when they got off, like I was an old-person kicker.

Which I am.

It took us about half an hour to get to Skipley, bouncing across the dales and moors. Yorkshire people have a lot of sticks. Almost everyone who got on the bus had a stick.

Skipley was a biggish town, it had cafés and shops and everything.

I said, "Look! These shops have got stuff in them. Not just boiled sweets. Other stuff."

We spent a lot of time trying on lipstick testers. I got

a blusher; well, more like little goldy pink balls that you brushed on. I noticed that a lot of the girls in the shop were very orange. And quite big. I was almost squashed to death when two of them reached for the same perfume as me.

We messed around most of the afternoon and got to the bus stop to go back at about six o'clock. The girls at Dother Hall had to be back by seven thirty unless they got written permission from Sidone, and then you had to say who you were going with and where.

Flossie said, "It'll be fun when you come up to the Hall to stay, Vaisey, although not necessarily for you, because Bob is making your bed."

The bus arrived. We piled on and just as we were about to go a group of lads came skittering around the corner and leapt on, too. I recognized Phil and Charlie, and as they came down the bus they saw us. Jo started fiddling about with her hair.

Phil said loudly, "Hurrah, it's the Tree Sisters. Are you having a thespian outing?"

The people on the bus started tutting. I went bright red, I think. I could feel my head on fire. Phil and Charlie sat down in the seats in front of Jo and me. And the other three went near Flossie and Vaisey. As the bus lurched off, Phil leaned over the back of his seat.

He said, "I still dream about our day in the woods."

I said, "It wasn't your day in the woods, it was our day

in the woods. And anyway, it wasn't our day in the woods, we were getting ideas."

Charlie popped his head up then and looked really closely at us.

"Was your idea to go and get off with trees?"

Jo hit him over the head with her Topshop bag.

Phil said, "I like a fight on the way home."

It was all getting a bit, I don't know, sort of tense, but I don't know why. The other boys were talking to Vaisey. And Flossie was talking to a bloke and his sheepdog. The bus stopped in the middle of nowhere. Not at a stop or anything, and a big old man got on and came up the bus toward us. He was carrying a chicken. It wasn't dead.

He looked at the boys leaning over the backs of the seats and said, "Ay, you young larrikins. Sit down properly, tha's not at home now."

Then he gave the chicken to a woman at the back and said, "Now then, that's for thee, bring us up any spare cow tit you've got and we'll call it evens."

She said, "Awreet, thanks, love."

Then the chicken man walked slowly down the bus and got off.

Somebody shouted out from the back, "Can't tha go a bit slower, at this rate I'll still be alive by the time we get to Heckmondwhite. Bloody hell."

When we shuddered off again, Phil popped his head up.

He looked at Jo.

She said, "What do you want?"

And he said, "Do you want to come to the pictures with me?"

I have never seen someone look so much like a human goldfish as Jo.

Eventually because he went on looking at her she said, "What?"

Phil went on, "Cinema, you and me, jogging boy and tree girl. Go on. Be a devil. Go on."

Jo was saying, "But I . . . don't . . ."

Then Charlie popped his head up.

"Go on, lady. Don't upset him. He's shy."

All the way home Jo has been driving us mad. How many times can you go through a conversation? A lot, is the answer.

We had to hang around at the bus stop for ages while she went on and on.

Jo said, "What does he mean, do you want to come to the pictures with me?"

Flossie said, "I'll tell you what he means. That *he wants to take you to the cinema.*"

We all nodded.

I said, "That sums it up. Night, night."

Jo said, "OK, what if I do go with him and then that's it. He doesn't want to see me again. Because I am too small. Or can beat him at arm wrestling or whatever. What then? I will have been dumped just because I said I would go. Whereas, if I hadn't gone in the first place I would have been all right."

I don't like myself for this, but I felt a bit jealous of Jo. At least she had been asked to go to the cinema by a real boy.

Jo said, "Anyway, I don't think I fancy him. He's too short."

After the girls trudged off up the lane to Dother Hall, Vaisey said, "I'd be excited if I'd been asked out by a boy. I liked that other boy on the bus. He's called Jack, but he didn't say anything to me. He sort of looked like he was going to and then he didn't."

I put my arm around her. "I'm sure you will get a boyfriend."

Vaisey said, "Have you met anyone you like yet? Do you like Charlie?"

I laughed in a casual way and said, "Charlie?"

She said, "Oh, I just wondered. I thought he might have asked you to go to the cinema as well."

To tell the truth, that is what I had thought in a little faraway place in my mind. He seemed friendly and sort of happy to see me, but he hadn't said anything. Why should he? He was quite a good-looking boy. Probably had a few girlfriends before.

I said to Vaisey, "Maybe he doesn't go for the Irish broomstick type?"

Vaisey said, "You're silly. Anyway, Honey said we had to show our glory."

I said, "I am showing my glory, look at me showing my glory." And I bent down and kissed my kneecaps as we walked along.

We had breakfast in the pub the next day. It was quite good fun being in a real pub when it was all secret and closed up. Especially as Ruby's dad had gone to the beer fest up in the dales. For a laugh, I was offering one of the stuffed deer a little sausage when a male voice said, "Hello, Tallulah."

I whirled round, hiding the sausage. It was Alex. Matilda went mad leaping up and down at his shins.

I said, "Hello, Alex." In a low voice, like the woman in James Bond. I don't know why.

Vaisey said, "Hi, Alex. I'm going to go in and work on my song. Laters."

Ruby went after her saying, "Vaisey, I want to show you Matilda's new collar, it lights up. Come and see, Lullah."

And she scampered off after Vaisey.

I was about to follow them when Alex said, "Come and sit in the sun with me. I haven't really heard about how you are getting on at college or anything."

I looked at him.

He was being quite nice, wasn't he? Was he?

We went and sat on the wall that ran around the grave-yard. You could see for miles from there and the moors looked green and not glowering like they often did. I could see big birds swooping and diving above the crags, like in *Wuthering Heights* on a good day. I felt warm in the sun and it was really nice sitting there with him. I was still nervous, because he was just so gorgeous. Like a film star, really. I don't think I had ever spoken to a grown-up boy before. About myself.

He said, "What do you like best about college, Tal-lulah?"

"Oh, I don't know really, I feel like I'm being me. Not that that is probably the best choice but . . ."

And he laughed. "What would be wrong with you?"

And that's when I did it.

"Oh, you know, the knee thingy. And the—" And just in time I stopped myself from saying the corkers word. I had very nearly said, to the best-looking boy in the uni-verse, "Alex, I haven't got any corkers, do you think they will ever grow?" And possibly followed that up by saying, "I have been trying various methods of corker-rubbing, what do you think?"

He was still reeling from the knee thingy.

"The knee thingy?"

I said, "Oh, I . . . well . . . they . . ."

He was looking at my jeans, where the knees would

be (in any ordinary-size legs). "What is wrong with your knees?"

He was looking at me, waiting for an answer. And half smiling.

I said, "It's just . . . that . . . they . . . are too far . . . up."

He laughed. "Too far up? Let me feel."

What????

I got off the wall and started backing away from him.

He said, "Go on."

I lost control then and said quite loudly, "Forget it. You will never see the knees."

And then he laughed and I started laughing as well. It was so ridiculous.

Just then Lavinia and Dav and Noos came pootling along on their bikes. They stopped when they saw us. Lavinia said, "Hi, Tallulah. Oiright? Top of the morning to you."

She looked at Alex properly and you could almost see her eyes going "wow." He did have the "wow" factor.

Then she said to Alex, "Oh, hi. Sorry to interrupt, I don't think we've met."

He said, "No, I think I would probably have remembered."

And she laughed. And looked at him again. Like Honey said you should. Right in the eyes and also for a bit too long.

Oh no. She liked him.

Alex said, "So are you all at Dother Hall? I might be coming up soon, I know Monty and he's giving me a bit of coaching."

Noos, clearly impressed, said, "Oh, are you an actor, then?"

Alex said, "I'd like to be, I've got a place at Liverpool next year."

Lavinia said, "I'm surprised you are talking to us, then."

And she smiled, and Alex said, "Are you?" In a sort of strange meaningful way which I didn't really get.

Then I got it, because Lavinia said, "Well, come and look for me when you come up to the college. It would be nice to see you."

And Alex said, "And it would be nice to see you."

And then there was another pause.

It was like being in *Alice in Wonderland* again. But I wasn't Alice. Once more I was the playing card. At the back.

In my squirrel room I lay on my bed with my squirrel slippers on. It seems like a really mean world, where some people get born with average knees and proper corkers and some people can't even find a category for their head in a magazine. Like me.

I am so miserable.

And alone.

I couldn't hang around at The Blind Pig watching Alex and Lavinia get off with each other. And the others are all off practicing for their assessment. I should practice as well, but apart from limbering up my knees, what could I do?

I'm hopeless.

I'm hopeless.

I'm going to be on the train home in a few days.

Then I heard the door open and a lot of hooting and noise downstairs.

"Helllllooooo, house. Look, look, boys, the house is happy to see us. Sam, don't put your tadpoles on the— Oh dear."

The Dobbinses are back.

I heard a lot of running and scampering and then footsteps up the stairs.

Dibdobs said through the door, "Tallulah . . . helloooo. We're back. . . . We've got lots of things to show you. . . . The boys wanted to say good night to you. Didn't you, boys?"

I heard them saying, "Eth."

Dibdobs was wearing a special outfit, knitted out of bits of string. I couldn't help staring at it.

She sort of blushed. "It's nice, isn't it? Unusual."

I said, "Yes, it is very unusual."

"Harold made it for me on his Iron Man weekend."

I should have stopped myself, but I said, "What are

Iron Man weekends? Does he go ironing, for the week-end?"

She laughed and snorted. "Lullah is being a silly billy, isn't she, boys?"

They blinked at me. Max said, "Shitty billy."

Dibdobs went even more red. "No, darling, it's SILLY Billy."

Sam said, "SHITTY Billy."

Dibdobs manically started stroking his hair down into an even more puddingy style. She said, "No, it's not an ironing weekend, worse luck!!!! It's when men go away together to find themselves. In the woods."

Men finding themselves in the woods, well, why were they having to do that when they must have gone to the woods in the first place? Apparently it's something to do with sweat lodges and living off the land. I didn't want the picture of Harold in a sweat lodge in my head.

Dibdobs said, "My dress is mostly made of leftover bits of string."

Lovely.

I said, "Well, good night, boys."

And the boys blinked back at me. Max came and hugged one of my knees. I even found myself ruffling his bowl head.

At least he likes my knees.

Dibdobs said, "Are you all right, Tallulah? Are you missing home a bit?"

Actually, I suppose I was, but anyway I was going to be back there soon.

I said, "No, it's just . . . you know . . ."

She said, "Growing up?"

Oh great balls of fire, was I growing even more?

Dibdobs said to me, "You need a big hug."

And she gave me one.

Then she said, "We're going off to read our book, aren't we, boys? Tell Tallulah who it's about."

"Bogie."

Dibdobs went puce.

"Now, boys, we've stopped using that silly word, because we are BIG boys now, aren't we?"

Max said, "Sjuuge boys."

Dibdobs laughed nervously. "All right, darling, HUGE boys, and huge boys know that the book we are reading is . . . *Alice in Wonderland*, isn't it?"

The boys nodded, and Max said, "Wiv a smiley cat!!"

Dibdobs laughed like he had just built an electricity pylon single-handedly. "Yes, tell Lullah about the Cheshire Cat."

And both of them smiled at me in the maddest way you have ever seen. Like their whole heads were one big mouth.

As she shooed them away, Sam turned round and took his dodie out. "Sjuuge cat, in Bogie bogie in Wunnerlant."

★ ★ ★

About an hour later, I was still tossing and turning and thinking how unfair everything was when there was a knock at my door again. It was my new "dad" this time. Harold had a little book in his hand.

"When I was at the Iron Man camp we did a lot of talking around the campfire. You know, men don't often get to reveal their softer side. And reading stories to each other as we lay around in the loincloths we had woven was revealing."

Oh nooo. He wasn't going to come and read a book to me, was he?

He had a dressing gown on and a pipe.

He fiddled in his pocket. Oh no, was he going to offer me a pipe as well, like they did round the campfire?

He held up the book and said, "Thought you might be interested in this," and gave it to me. Then he left.

I may as well read it a bit.

I might be able to get some ideas for a performance out of it.

At least it will stop me thinking about Lavinia and Alex—and Cain. The book was called *Heathcliff: Saint or Sinner—Really Bad or Just Really Upset?*

Oh no. No. This is not going to help me cheer up. I am going to write some of my own stuff in my performance-art notebook.

Hmmmm.

★ ★ ★

Two lost travelers are on the moors, near the dreaded Grimbottom, when suddenly a thunderstorm breaks. The rain is pelting down and lightning splits the sky.

They hear something terrible howling (note to self—is it Dr. Light-howler?) and they start running. The howling gets nearer. One of them falls over and then—Gadzooks and Lordy Lordy—they see lights. And hear a piano.

The welcoming lights of an old inn. The sign creaks in the howling wind. A flash of lightning illuminates the sign. On it is a piggy in dark glasses with a walking stick.

They stagger in out of the howling, terrifying storm. Everyone in the bar stops talking and stares at them. The pianist gets his coat and leaves. A clock ticks loudly. A stuffed stag's head falls off the wall.

One of the travelers, the one with the nobbly knees (me) says, "Oh—hello, we've come to Yorkshire by mistake."

And the landlord with two pies in his hands says, "You're not from around here, are thee?"

The other traveler, the one with fluffy hair and a sticky-up nose (Vaisey) says, "No, no—we are looking for Dother Hall, we are artists."

Everyone laughs.

The landlord says, "But are you mime artists?"

I nod, twice.

Vaisey says, "And I do a bit of tap. We mean no harm, we just want to don our tights and tap-dance our way to the top."

I say, "Yes, yes, we want to live forever, we want to learn how to fly!!"

Everyone stares at us.

I say desperately, "Look! We can prove it! We are wearing our new all-in-one dance bodies-and-leggings underneath our kagouls."

The burly landlord says, "Put them in the room with the others."

We are led to a door and when it opens we see . . . the room is full of performance art students. Some in all-in-one body-and-leggings dancewear.

A few just in leggings. Some of them are very old.

Walking to college with Vaisey, I said, "It will be a relief to get back to the Dother ship." I was wrong.

Jo was waiting for us by the gates because she's had a note from Phil, asking her to meet him outside M & S on Wednesday to see a film called *Night of the Vampire Bats*.

Jo showed us his note:

This film makes Twilight seem like afternoon.

Jo said, "Look, and this is where you two come in."

Bring two others, for my mates. Phil.

Jo looked at me and Vaisey.

I said, "No."

Jo went on and on all day. It was driving me mad.

Everywhere I looked she was doing her saddy face.

When I went to the loo she was there outside the loo door, looking at me like a sad puppy. Not even saying anything.

The trouble was that Vaisey had said she would go, "just for a laugh," but I think she is hoping that Jack would be going. So it was all right for her. Flossie and Honey are off the hook because they have extra singing that night.

I finally gave in when Jo gave me an apple with a little crying face carved in it.

Night of the Vampire Bats

I DON'T KNOW WHY I am so bothered about this "date."

I'm not even officially on the date.

We had to go and try and get permission from Sidone to go to the cinema at nighttime. She was in her inner chamber, um, I mean office. She was lying down on a chaise longue with a cup of tea.

"Darlings, I am ex-hausted. I had a call from a friend directing *Cats* and he has bled me dry. I have practically redesigned the whole thing lying on this chaise longue. Sit, sit."

We sat, sat.

"It beggars belief that he would only realize he didn't have enough cat costumes the day before he opens. They can be an ugly, demanding crowd in Cleckheaton. I know, I gave my Ophelia there and someone called the social services. Sometimes this profession is a tyranny. Still, darlings, you came to see me for something?"

I said, "We'd like to go to the cinema in Skipley on Wednesday night, because we were thinking that for the lunchtime performance we could, um, use some of the ideas and themes from the film."

She was very, very interested. Unfortunately. And swept her hair back. "What are you thinking? What is this germ, this shoot you are nurturing? Is it an interior idea? What is the film?"

And Jo said, "Well . . . it's called . . . *Night of the Vampire Bats.*"

She said, "Yes, and what is it about?"

Jo said helpfully, "It's set at night."

Sidone was looking into the distance and twirling her earrings. "Ah, the night. The mysterious, shadowy underworld that covers so many, many broken dreams."

I thought she was going to start crying, she was so moved by her broken dreams.

Jo stumbled on, "But, but, really I think it's about . . . um . . . an interior darkness."

I was just about to say, "That bats must feel because they can't see much." But luckily Sidone stood up.

"Marvelous! I utterly see where you are going with this. . . . It's the long dark night of the soul, isn't it?"

I was inwardly thinking, You can say that again, but outwardly saying, "Um."

Anyway, we are allowed to go. Amazingly.

As we came out of her office, she shouted after us, "Strive, strive for authenticity, my dears. Even when you feel the cold tremors of fear and bleakness tearing and biting at your heels."

As we closed the door to her inner sanctum, I said, "I think I can feel my feet beginning to bleed quite a lot."

I was exhausted from lying. I'm so useless at it.

Vaisey said to Jo, "You said that *Night of the Vampire Bats* was about interior darkness."

I said, "Well, it will be. It's really dark in the cinema."

Jo was pleased because we had got away with it. She shook her little head and said, "Yes, OK, it is about bats . . . but mostly . . . it's . . . about my very first date!!!!"

I said bitterly, "It's all right for you, but me and Vaisey don't know if we are officially on a date or just part of an away-day package supersaver. Three for the price of one."

Jo looked up at both of us and said, "I know you are doing this for me, and I'd just like to say thank you, my new friends."

And she gave us a friendly biff on the arm to show how very pleased she was.

For a small girl she packs quite a punch.

As we strolled to the gates to go home, I shouted back, "Didn't you say that Phil is too small for you?"

Jo shouted back like I was a bit thick, "Tallulah, it's the cinema. We'll be sitting down."

★ ★ ★

The next evening, I met Vaisey in the dressing room of life. Otherwise known as Vaisey's room in The Blind Pig. Even though I am on a not-really-date, I am still nervous.

I have makeup on and Vaisey has made my hair go va-va-voom with her hair dryer. Anyway, now Vaisey and Ruby want me to try a red dress on. It's Vaisey's and she says it's too long for her.

I said, "No, I don't wear dresses."

They both went on and on, and Ruby even made Matilda lift her paw up and look at me.

As if she was saying in dog language, "Please put the dress on, otherwise I may never eat another bonio treat again."

It was pathetic. But it worked, because in the end I agreed to at least try on the dress. I went behind the door. It was a bit tight getting it on.

I said, "It's too small for me. I can't lift my arms up."

Vaisey said, "Come out and show us."

Ruby said, "You've left your cardigan and jeans on."

I said, "It's all the rage."

She said, "No, it's not. You look like the Sheriff of Nottingham."

I said, "I have to have them . . . on . . . in case I get cold."

Ruby said, "Take them off. Now."

In the end I went behind the door and took off my stuff

and put on the dress. When I came out I could see myself in the mirror.

The dress came to midthigh. Which in normal legs would mean a third of the way down your leg. In my case, it meant that it was an eighth of the way down my leg.

No one actually said anything at first, they just looked at my legs—even Matilda.

Then Ruby said, "I think it looks brill."

Vaisey was nodding.

Matilda was nodding, too. But it may be fleas.

Then Ruby suddenly said, "Oy, you're getting lady bumps!!! I can see 'em."

What what???

I put my arms over my front.

"Ooooooh, give us a look."

I said, "I'm not a horse. You'll be feeling my fetlocks in a minute."

In fact Ruby did try to feel them.

I wanted to skip around shouting, "I've got corkers!" But I didn't, because Ruby would quite likely yell downstairs to her dad.

But I am deeply down secretly thrilled.

I am so very right to keep up my secret rubbing practices.

When we were ready I told Ruby, "Now you cannot sneak out with us and sit in the back row, spying for a laugh."

On our way out to catch the bus we passed Mr. Barra-clough in the bar combing the hair of one of his stuffed stags. He had given it a center parting, which is not respect-ful of a noble breed. But I didn't say.

He did glance up as we passed and said to Ruby, "Where's the other big lad gone?"

And then he looked at me and said, "Oh, there you are."

I said to Ruby, "It's very hard to think that your dad, is, well, Alex's dad. Alex not around, then?"

Ruby rolled her eyes.

When we got to the bus stop Jo was there waiting for us. Hopping about. Which was a bit odd because she was also sitting on the wall.

She looked lovely. All shiny and dark. Mad, but shiny and dark also. She was wearing a wrapover top and a rough-cut denim skirt with wedgie shoes. And a lot of bangles and necklaces.

She said, "Do I look all right? Would you snog me?"

I said, "What? Now?"

And me and Ruby and Vaisey laughed.

But Jo wasn't in a laughy mood.

She was in an "I've gone mad" mood.

On and on. Is he too short? Am I too short? What is too short??

Ruby said, "Jo, if I were thee, I'd stick to smiling a lot.

And shut your gob for the rest of the time. See thee later. Vaisey, make sure you tell me all about it."

The bus came and we got on. And it was only then that I thought of something.

"What if they get on at the next stop? That's where they got off last time. What if they get on and we have to do sitting-down hello for the first time? How do you do sitting-down hello?"

In the end we were so hysterical that we went to the back of the bus and crouched down in our seats. Then Vaisey started singing the theme tune to *Doctor Who* as we drew near to the dreaded bus stop.

As it happened, they didn't get on.

But it had left us all even more jittery.

Vaisey said, "Maybe they jogged to Skipley?"

I said, "I don't think so. Phil and Charlie had to have a lie down for five minutes after they started running, if you remember?"

We were bouncing along, and the bus driver had been shouting stuff about the places we were passing. Even though we didn't ask him to. Even though nobody asked him to.

Stuff like, "On your left you will notice the free-range egg sign. Old Stoat Farm do a range of free-range products that cannot be beat. The bearded couple who own it, from Leeds I believe, sleep in the same barn as the hens, in case the hens have a nasty dream. That is how caring and stupid townsfolk can be."

Just as we passed Grimbottom, he shouted, "That randy bull's at it again."

Vaisey had been applying lip gloss for most of the journey.

I said, "Vaisey, how much lip gloss can you get on? You'll never be able to get off the bus at this rate."

Jo was looking in her compact mirror and fiddling about with her hair.

She said, "I don't even know why I am doing this. He might not be able to see my hair. Where do you think he comes up to on me?" And she stood up swaying around on the bus.

She said, "Do you think he would come up to my ears?"

I said, "Shut up about your ears. At least you know who you're meeting. What about me and Vaisey? We're just the 'two others.'"

I was chatting for chatting's sake really, to keep my mind off imagining Phil's friend who might be my date. I wouldn't mind if it was Charlie. And Phil and Charlie are mates. And Charlie liked my knees. But what if Charlie came and preferred Vaisey?

That would be a double blow. Unless the other one that wasn't him was dreamy.

But whatever happened, neither one of them was going to be Alex.

Alex was out of my league.

I wasn't even in a league.

To him I was just another little fourteen-and-a-half-year-old. He probably couldn't tell the difference between one fourteen-and-a-half-year-old and another, they all looked the same to him. Stupid.

The bus finally juddered to a halt at the M & S stop and we got off. There was no one there. Well, apart from a woman in headscarf and Wellingtons.

She got on the bus and the bus driver said, "Mary Bottomly, you are a dream come true. A vision of beauty in a world of—"

She cuffed him on his cap and said, "Don't bloody start, I've just had some cow heel and it's made my bloody lips stick together like superglue."

I said to the other two, "This is no place for artists. Look, why don't we just get a Coke and catch the next bus back before—"

And then we saw Phil and Jack and . . . someone who was not Charlie, bowling toward us. I wish I had my jeans on; my legs were feeling very shy and exposed. They hadn't been out much.

Phil whistled at us and said, "Oy oy!"

Jack and "the other one" were grinning, but not saying anything. This might be a very long night, and I was already longing to be tucked up with my squirrel slippers.

Phil said, "This is Jack, you met him before on the bus, and this is Ben. Ben is excellent at all sorts of sport. Aren't you, Ben?"

Ben was nodding and smiling now.

He had floppy hair and it was going up and down.

Ben was quite good-looking, a bit on the floppy-hair side. But tall.

As we went along to the cinema the boys were walking ahead, sort of stopping and turning round and making jokes to one another.

Vaisey said quietly to me, "Lullah, can I have Jack?"

What is the right answer to that?

I said, "That would mean that I had Ben."

And Vaisey said, "He's quite tall."

I said, "I KNOW he's quite tall. Tallness isn't everything."

Jo said, "You can say that again. Don't you like Ben?"

I said, "I don't know."

Then, as if he had heard us, Ben turned round and looked at me. Then he turned back and said something to Jack.

Oh God. Perhaps he was doing the same. Perhaps he was saying stuff about me.

I wanted to run away.

When we got to the cinema the boys paid for the tickets and we went into the dark. Phil chose a row of seats about middle way up. I could see there was a snoggers' row at the back. At least Phil hadn't chosen that row.

He went first and said to Jo, "Why don't you sit next to me, in case I get fwightened?"

Jo giggled in a girlish, slightly hysterical way that I had never heard before. I hoped she wasn't going to turn from a rufty-tufty girl into an idiot.

Then Jack sat a couple of seats away from Jo and smiled at Vaisey. He patted the empty seat next to him.

So, that left me and Ben.

But Ben didn't move.

Should I go and sit down? Or run out of the cinema?

Maybe he would run out of the cinema.

Or maybe go and sit miles away from me because he was so alarmed by my knees.

Perhaps if I fainted and—

Then Ben said, "Tallulah, why don't you go in first? And then I can protect you."

I hadn't heard him speak before and his voice was a bit croaky.

I smiled and shook my hair and we went and sat down.

What was he going to be protecting me from?

A violent ice-cream lady?

Then the film began. *Night of the Vampire Bats* was very . . . what's the right word? Batty. I wasn't really watching it because I was so tense, I thought I might be sick. That would be attractive.

Ben was silent, and I daren't catch his eye. I just held my head rigidly forward.

What was everyone else doing? I swiveled my eyes as far as they would go without moving my neck and could sort of see Phil and Jo in the flickering half-light.

I think Phil might have had his arm around Jo. But it could have been someone's leg from the row behind. I couldn't see Jack and Vaisey's arms, but they could have been doing secret handy-holding.

Ben had his arm on the armrest so I kept my hands in my lap. Should I move one hand closer to him so that it was more easily accessible?

Did I want him to hold my hand?

I didn't know.

What I did know was that I didn't want him to not want to hold my hand. If you see what I mean.

Halfway through the film and still nothing had happened. If I didn't move my neck soon it would snap off.

Ben leaned toward me and said something so softly I couldn't hear him.

I whispered back, "Sorry, what did you say?"

And I thought he said, "Do you want a squeeze?"

A squeeze.

Nobody had mentioned that to me before.

Was a squeeze the same as a hug?

Because hugging was what you did to teddies, not girl-friends, wasn't it?

I could sense him waiting for me to reply, so I said very quietly in his ear, or where I thought his ear might be under his floppy hair, "I don't think I know you well enough."

And then he said a bit more loudly, "They're still in the bag, I haven't touched them."

Pardon?

And he held out a bag of Maltesers.

Did I want a Malteser.

I don't know you well enough.

Oh goodie! Now he knows I'm tall and an idiot.

The cinema experience was the longest, tensest hour and a half of my life, so far.

When at last we came out of the cinema, we got chips and walked across to the bus stop to eat them. Because we were all holding the bags everyone's hands were in full sight. So there was no arm-around business going on.

When the bus came, Mary Bottomly in the headscarf and Wellingtons was driving. She had her headscarf on underneath her official cap. And she didn't have a smiley jolly bus-driver face.

Phil led the way to the back of the bus and sat down in the window seat.

We followed him and when we got to the back seat,

Phil said, "Whey hey hey," and pulled Jo down onto his knee. For once, she was speechless and just sat there like a mad doll.

I didn't know what to say or where to sit.

Vaisey and Jack sat down next to each other and Jack started showing her his harmonica. To my amazement, she looked "interested." Maybe that is what you had to do, look interested when boys talked. Even about harmonicas.

So that leaves me.

With Ben.

Ben was easy to talk to—if you like talking about what type of running shoes are best for cross-country. It was quite relaxing, just half listening to him.

Then I heard Jack say the word "guitar." And Vaisey's head started nodding in agreement and she was talking as well. Must be about music.

How sweet. I think Jack's a bit shy, but I think he likes Vaisey. Then they started singing together and Jack was making a drumming rhythm on his knees.

Phil was now tickling Jo, who was going mental. And screeching. So much so that Mrs. Bottomly, the driver, yelled back, "Oy, stop playing silly beggars. This is a bloody bus, not a Mardi Gras!!"

Oooh, now Ben is telling me about how he does pull-ups because he's a bit weak in the upper arm. And apparently upper-arm strength is a big plus when you want to join the navy. And he does want to join the navy.

He said, "When we do our cross-country runs I put bricks in my rucksack."

Just to be nice, I said, "Crikey."

The boys didn't get off at their stop because Phil said, "We'll escort you ladeez to your homes in case of carriages going by and sloshing your evening gowns."

What is he talking about?

Phil said, "We've been doing Jane Austen at Woolfe, so we can get inside the female mind."

I said, "What is inside our female minds, then?"

Phil said, "Well, for instance, should one of you want to climb up a staircase on the way home, we lads would have the training to quickly get behind you and walk up the stairs, bracing ourselves."

I said, "Bracing yourselves for what?"

Phil winked. "Aaaa, bracing ourselves for the moment when you lost your footing, or fainted, and then we could catch you, saving you from injury."

I said, "Why would we faint?"

And Phil said, "You might be startled by bats."

And everyone laughed.

We said "good night" to the bus-driver woman as we got off.

And she said, "Is it?"

I don't think she likes people, as such.

As the bus careered into the distance, there was a bit

of an awkward silence.

We were all still standing by the bus stop.

So I said to everyone, "Well, I'm off to my squirrel room. Thanks for the cinema, and the, um, Maltesers. It's been, um, quite smashing."

And I set off for the Dobbinses'.

I'd gone a few yards when Ben came after me. "I'll walk you to your gate, Tallulah."

He looked up from under his floppy fringe and said, "I had a nice night, it was really interesting talking to you."

There was more silence as we crossed the village green, so I said, "Um, do you like theater as well as running and so on? Like we do at Dother Hall?"

He looked at me like I had spoken in ancient bee language. And repeated, "Theater . . ."

I said, to lighten the moment, "Ms. Beaver says it's a harsh mistress and your feet bleed before you put on the golden slippers of applau—"

And I'd just got to "applause" when he put his hand on my shoulder and turned me round to face him.

I was about to take a piece of hair out of my mouth, because as he spun me round my hair went a bit wild. But he lunged at me, mouthfirst.

He put the whole of his mouth on mine. My eyes were open so I could see that he had his closed. His mouth seemed very big. In fact, I felt like I was being eaten. Even though no chewing was going on.

141

I had to breathe through my nose because he was blocking my mouth.

Then I felt a little proddy thing going in between my lips like it was trying to prise them open. Was there still a bit of hair in there?

Or maybe he had trapped his fringe.

It was very floppy and . . .

My goodness, it must be his tongue.

What was I supposed to do?

The prodding was still going on. I had my teeth together because I was so tense.

The little jabby tongue thing started working its way along my toothline.

It prodded at the side of my mouth, which was tickly, actually.

I don't think laughing would go down well, though.

In fact, it was like being in *Night of the Vampire Bats*. There was a bit in the film where a bat flew into someone's mouth, and you could see it barging around inside because the cheeks kept bulging out, and the bat's little head popped out now and then.

Perhaps I should move my lips a bit.

Or perhaps now was the time to turn my head away and look through the window and say, "Not now," in a low voice. Except that there wasn't a window and . . .

Then he just stopped and said, "Er, sorry, about that, erm . . . well, good night." And he held out his hand.

I had had my arms by my side for the whole time and I put my hand up automatically.

And he shook it.

Then the worst thing happened. Well, another worst thing happened. Cain came round the corner. With a dead fox in his hand. He'd probably killed it for a little snack. He looked at us from under his black hair. I think he might have black eyes as well. And he was dressed all in black. He just stopped and looked at us, twirling the dead fox.

Ben said, a bit nervously, I thought, "Well, I'll, er . . . see you around, Tallulah."

Cain just looked at him and said as he went off, "Ay, off you go, garyboy. Dunt make me leery because things might get a bit gory."

What did that mean?

Then he looked at me. Just looked. I didn't know what to do.

He looked me slowly up and down and then half smiled, but not in a jolly "ooooh what a laugh everything is" way. It was sort of spooky.

He turned to go off down the lane, but looked back and said, "Now we're evens. Tha's caught me snogging and now I've caught thee snogging."

I never seem to know what to say to Cain.

I said, "I wasn't snogging."

And he said, "No, and you weren't cleaning your windows either."

As he walked off twirling his fox, I thought, next time I'll think of something really clever to say to him.

The Dobbinses were in the kitchen when I went in. But the twins were in bed so I was saved the staring interlude.

Harold was in an "interested" mood and he asked me about the film.

"What was the genre?"

I said, "Um, bats mostly."

Harold loved bats, unfortunately.

I knew that because he got his pipe out.

Which, incidentally, he never lights, he just sucks it and points with it.

"Most fascinating creatures . . . I think I may have a stuffed one in a drawer."

Never mind the bats, I have had my first kiss. From a boy.

I escaped from the bat chamber into my squirrel room where I lay down on my bed next to my squirrel slippers and gave them a little hug. It was a full moon and I heard an owl hooting. Probably Connie, hanging about waiting for the birth of her owl twins. Eating rodents to keep her mind off motherhood.

I feel somehow changed.

Not like a werewolf. Fur isn't growing on the back of

my hands. Although it might be growing under my arm-pits, at last.

I am no longer a child. My corkers are emerging, and I've had my first kiss.

I've had my first taste of bat—I mean romance.

As a mark of my new being, I put the squirrel slippers on the floor.

I will no longer have cuddly-toy type things near me.

Whooo-hoo-oooo

VAISEY WAS WAITING FOR me in the kitchen when I came down next morning.

She was nodding and pretending to be interested in what the twins had made at playschool. Dibdobs said it was a vase. But to me it was a washing-up-liquid bottle cut in half, with what looked like snot all over it.

As I was eating my toast, Vaisey kept raising her eyebrows at me. She said, "We should go, Lullah, we . . . need to get limbered up. "

Now it was my turn to raise my eyebrows.

She said, "You know, the performance lunchtime thingymajig."

I said, "The performance lunchtime thingymajig?"

She said, "Yes."

I said, "Hmm . . . OK."

Dibdobs said, "Oooo, that sounds interesting, what is it about?"

I said, "Yeah. Good point. What is it about, Vaisey?"

Vaisey looked like she had swallowed a whole shoe. Just then Harold came into the kitchen with a fishing net and wearing thigh-length boots.

"Morning, campers! And what a glorious morning it is. I'm going to take the boys fishing. Come on, Sam and Max, welligogs on and tricycles out!!!"

And he rootled around in the hall cupboard and brought out two wooden tricycles. The boys started making chuffing noises.

Dibdobs smiled. "Oooh, you boys think it's like Thomas the Tank Engine, but it's not a train, is it, boys? What is it?"

Sam said, "Sjuuuge."

Dibdobs was determined that although her boys might look like idiots, they were not going to be calling tricycles trains.

"Yes, it's a huge . . . tricycle, isn't it?"

They just went on huffing and tooting.

Then Harold popped back in to say, "Come on, boys, split splot! Look, Daddy's got his tricycle ready to go as well."

We looked beyond him into the garden and there it was. His tricycle.

After they had all gone Dibdobs said, "Sorry, girls,

you were telling me about your performance, how exciting! What did you say it was about?"

I looked at Vaisey, she looked at me, and I blurted, "It's a . . . bicycle ballet."

A bicycle ballet?

Actually it sounded quite good.

Dibdobs said, "A bicycle ballet? Gosh, that sounds good. How does it work? What happens?"

I said, "Well . . . it's a ballet . . . done on bicycles. Come on, Vaisey, we must go and, er . . . polish our saddles and so on."

Vaisey said as soon as we got out the door, "So, so, what happened???"

I looked thoughtful.

I was thoughtful.

The trouble is I didn't know what I thought.

What had happened?

I said, "You go first."

Vaisey's hair had gone completely mad. She had not strapped it down under a hat or tied it half to death with a lacky band and it was taking full advantage. Bobbing around. Sticking up on end. She looked like an electrified floor mop.

We ambled up round the village green and toward the bridge to go to Dother Hall.

She said, "Well, in the cinema, we sat down, didn't

we? And it was all dark, and I daren't look to see what anyone else was doing."

I said, "I know my eyes nearly fell out trying to look out of the corners. I think that Phil put his arm around Jo."

Vaisey said, "I think he did."

I said, "I mean, I thought it was his arm, but then I thought it might have been the leg of someone in the row behind, sort of sticking up."

Vaisey said, "There wasn't anyone in the row behind. The only people were about three rows back and you would have had to have eight-foot legs to reach—"

Then her gaze sort of drifted to my legs.

I said, "Go on."

"Well, about halfway through, Jack shifted his legs a bit and one of them brushed against my knee. I looked round at him and he smiled at me."

Wow. I said, "Yabba dabba dooooo . . . here we go. Then what happened?"

She said, "That was it."

"OK, well go from the bit when I left."

Vaisey shook her hair about.

"Well, we all chatted for a bit and then Phil said he would walk Jo home."

I said, "Oh yes, I see. Walking her home. Leaving you all alone with Jack the smiler."

I winked at her.

But she didn't see me, because she had walked in some sheep poo. So I said, "And? When they went, you did a bit more smiling, and then—"

"We talked about stuff."

"You talked about stuff and then—"

Vaisey looked at me. "He showed me his new plectrum. But said he really wanted to be a drummer."

"And then he lunged—"

"No, then he said good night, thanks, see you later. Do you think that's bad? Do you think it means he doesn't really like me? Except in a musical sense?"

She looked a bit upset and her hair had gone flat. "Anyway, I like him. What happened to you?"

I told her about the kiss thingy.

She looked at me like I was the cat's pajamas and said, "You have kissed a boy. In *person*."

I said, "Yeppity doo dah."

Vaisey said, "And what was it like?"

I said, "Well, um, it was a bit like being attacked by a jelly, and then having a little bat trapped in your mouth."

Vaisey said, "Was it nice? Did you like it? Did he like it?"

And I said, "Well, he shook my hand at the end."

When we arrived at Dother Hall there was a big notice on the board that said:

Summer School girls
Report to the main hall at 10:30 a.m.
For assessment meeting.

Whoops.

This was all getting a bit scary.

We loped in with the others and sat down. Gudrun came onto the stage with a chair and a drum and started beating a rhythm. The lights flashed and I could see Bob half concealed by the side curtains, at control center. Well, the lighting desk. He was crouched over a keyboard, moving dials and waggling stuff like a man possessed. It was only then we recognized they were playing a reggae version of "All Things Bright and Beautiful."

As the music reached a crescendo, Sidone appeared onstage, dressed in a suit and braces. She stood looking out at us.

Gudrun sidled off backward with her drum as Sidone began to speak.

"Girls, my girls. You have been here now at Dother Hall for nearly two weeks, finding your feet. Although Madame Frances tells me that some of you have two left ones!"

She laughed softly.

We laughed. What were we laughing at? Was she talking about me?

Sidone continued. *"Tranquil, mes enfants.* Of course

151

you have come here to experiment, to enjoy your art, but as I said, this is no life for the fainthearted. There are no free rides on the people-carrier of Fame."

Now she looked very serious indeed.

"Some of you will only have a single ticket. For you there will be no return journey."

Offstage we heard someone fall over a drum and loud swearing.

Sidone paid no heed.

"Next week's performance lunchtime marks the half-way period of your time here, and it is then that you will receive your assessment mark. This will go toward your final assessment. That is all."

As she began to walk toward the wings, she spoke again.

"Be alert, keep notebooks, seek out beauty and art where you can. Look around you and remember some of the greatest works of literature were written in these rolling landscapes. Work, work until your feet bleed."

As we surged out on our way to tap-dancing class, all us summer school girls were jabbering away.

Vaisey said, "I wonder how many of us they keep on? I'll die if I can't stay."

Jo said, "I don't know what I will do, if I can't come back."

Flossie said, "I haven't even thought what I would do, if I don't get on."

Neither had I.

But I was pretty sure I should be thinking. I had a horrible knot in my tummy.

As if the assessment thing wasn't bad enough, now we had another thing I had never done: tap.

I liked the little shoes we were given, with the tappy bits on. They made a nice noise.

Then Monty arrived. He said, "Madame Frances is indisposed, so I will be taking the tap class. We soldier on."

Where do men get those far-too-short shorts from? Surely no shop would sell them. He did have long woolly leg warmers on too, but that is not the point.

Some of us who hadn't done tap before had to do "shuffle–ball change" to "Bob the Builder" for forty minutes with Monty doing it in front of us.

With actions and lots of shouting.

"No, no, Tallulah. Shuffle, dear, shuffle. Try not to let your knees knock. And lift your arms up, dear. Like so . . . oh, mind Milly's head . . . are you all right, Milly? Up you get. Stand a bit farther away from Tallulah, she's longer than she realizes."

Vaisey, Honey, Jo, Flossie, and the others who could do tap got into a huddle whilst Monty "left them to it." At the end of the session they did a bit from a show called *West Side Story* to really fast music, where they were rival gangs having a knife fight while tap-dancing. It was amazing. Really tappy.

I was impressed by my new friends. They can actually do stuff.

At break we walked through the woods to our special tree.

I was dying to ask Jo what had happened with her and Phil.

When we sat down and got out our snacks, I said, "So what happened, then?"

And instead of answering, Jo was bouncing up and down on a tree trunk.

Just bouncing.

I said, "Did he kiss you?"

And she got up and ran around in a circle and then threw herself into a bush.

I said, "Can you just tell us in words what happened?"

And Jo got up onto a tree stump and started belting out, "I did it MYYYYYYYY WAY!!"

In the end, Vaisey and me grabbed hold of her and I said, "Will you tell us what happened?"

She said, "Well, you saw that he sat down and then, you know, said I should sit down, in case he got frightened. And we were sitting there, sort of watching the bats, only I wasn't really watching the bats because I was too excited. In fact, I think I may have gone momentarily blind. Well, then I felt this thing in the dark. Snaking around my shoulders."

Honey said, "The thnaking awound thing?"

Jo said, "Exactly. And it was his arm. At first it was on the back of the seat, but then it sort of snaked round my shoulders."

Vaisey said, "Tallulah thought it was somebody's leg."

Jo said, "What sort of a person would put their leg round your shoulders? In the cinema?"

I said, "It's only because I was squinty-eyed and couldn't see properly."

Jo said, "Anyway, you might not have noticed, but we held hands on the bus."

I said, "All I noticed was you bouncing around on Phil's knee and giggling."

Jo said, "Well, it's very soothing actually, sitting on someone's knee and them jogging you about. I was thinking he could be Mr. Darcy. And I could say, 'Oh, Mr. Darcy, I fear you are making fun of a poor London girl not used to country ways.'"

Vaisey said, quickly, "Well nothing much happened to me, but you tell, Lullah."

I felt a bit red. And my legs were aching. Pray God it wasn't growing pains.

Flossie said, "Go on. Tell."

I said, "Well . . . you know when you have your first snog, and it feels like a tiny bat is barging around in your mouth? Well, it felt like that."

They just looked at me.

Then Jo said, "Anyway, can I get on to serious stuff?

Phil walked back to Dother Hall with me. It was a dark, soft night, the moon blushing in the sky." She was leaning against the tree. Lost in Loveland.

"As we drew near to the gates of Dother Hall the old bell in the belfry rang out. I said, 'I must go in, it's nigh on ten of the clock.' He half turned away from me, his jacket collar hiding his expression. Was he angry? Disappointed?"

I said, "Hungry?"

Jo ignored me, but as she passed by acting out walking away from Phil, she allowed her hand to slap against my head.

"As I turned to enter the gates, feeling shaken and weak, I felt his hand on my arm." She mimed feeling his hand on her arm.

Flossie said, "It wasn't Bob, was it, out for a late-night rubbish run?"

Jo slapped her on her head as she passed.

Then in a soft voice she said, "And it was then that he gently pulled me toward him. I felt powerless to resist and he kissed me on the mouth."

Wooooooohoooooooooo.

Wooooo-hooo-hooooooo.

Just as things were about to get really good on the snogging information, there was a crunching twig sort of noise, and Phil and Charlie came slowly jogging into the copse.

I felt a bit shy seeing Charlie, I don't know why. I

wonder if he can tell that I have kissed someone. They both jogged on the spot for a minute, which I thought was very funny.

Charlie said, "Hey hey, Tree Sisters. Please let us lie down, we're pooped."

And they both flung themselves down under our tree. Phil winked at Jo.

"Did you get back into Dither Hall all right?"

Jo looked sort of pleased and pink and shy all at the same time. She didn't say anything. Just nodded. And did a high-pitched sort of snort.

Vaisey said, "Have you been made to go jogging again?"

Charlie said, "No, it's far, far worse than that. We're on a grueling six-mile run."

I felt a bit funny. Charlie was nice and seemed pleased to see us, but not particularly interested in me. When Phil was talking about the *Vampire Bats* thing and doing his impression of a vampire being attacked by bats (which looked like a mad teddy bear waving off some bees), Charlie said, "Yeah, Ben said you had a laugh."

What did he know?

Were boys like girls? Did they tell each other everything?

Maybe Ben had said, "Yes, that Tallulah was rubbish at kissing, she just stood there and pulled hair out off her mouth."

When Gudrun sounded her gong for the afternoon

sesh, Phil said to Jo, "We've been confined to barracks at nights."

Jo said, "Oh my God, what did you do?"

Charlie said, "A couple of the prefects, also known as the Posh Trevs, caught us accidentally juggling with West Riding otters."

We looked at them both.

Vaisey said, "Juggling is not a crime."

I said, "It should be."

And Charlie and Phil laughed.

I felt quite proud that they thought I had said something funny.

Flossie said, "Did you really juggle with otters?"

Charlie said, "Nah. But we did change a country sign on our marathon and the Posh Trevs rode their mountain bikes into the river."

Phil said, "Yeah, it's really, really serious . . . we are forbidden to go out after hours for the next week."

Jo looked a bit sad, even though she tried to hide it.

Then Phil said, "Or to put it another way, see you after college. Bye, small bouncy person."

And Jo blushed and bounced off proudly.

We had art all afternoon with Dr. Lightowler. I wasn't feeling great, because she hadn't really taken to me. But as we were waiting for her, Sidone swept into the studio, all in black—capri trousers, bolero top, and a matador hat. She stopped and looked at us.

"Girls, Dr. Lightowler is covering for Madame Frances with the lower sixth group. Madame Frances is, I am afraid, still a little under the weather. So . . . use the time to 'experiment' in different forms. There's paper, paints, chicken wire, plaster. . . . Think of where you are, think of what the experience of Dother Hall means to you."

Flossie did a sketch of a giant ironing board and iron that she's going to make out of chicken wire. Vaisey went off to do moody sketches of the dales and the clouds over Grimbottom. It was quite jolly having no one to tell us what to do.

Jo and Honey started singing and chatting.

Jo said, "I love it here now, I want to come and be here full-time, more than anything in the world."

Honey said, "It would be fun, to be here full-time weally. I weally hope and pway I get chothen to thtay. I hope we all do."

And she started singing, "Thomewhere over the wainbow faw-a-way."

And Jo joined in and they ended up standing on the desk singing, "Why, oh, why can't I?"

Originally, I thought of wrapping the whole of Dother Hall in brown paper. That would get me noticed. There is a French artist who does stuff like that. He wrapped up the White Cliffs of Dover in clingfilm, or something.

I don't know why, but I know I liked it. However, when I went and asked Bob where the brown paper was kept he said, "In Gudrun's top drawer."

So I had to think of something else on a smaller scale for the time being.

I decided to make a cover for my performance-art/summer-of-love notebook. I have collaged the front and back of it with a mixture of leaves and sheep's wool, and stuck on some bits of slate I found that had fallen off the roof.

To me it says "Yorkshire, the beginning of my dream."

I am going to pour my heart and soul into it.

All right, I can't dance or sing, but I have got something to offer, I know I have, and I don't mean my knees.

Gudrun came to tell Vaisey that her bed in the dorm was ready at last and that Bob will drive down later to get her stuff from The Blind Pig. Vaisey is really excited.

After the bell went, Vaisey and I walked home together, probably for the last time this summer.

Maybe forever.

We were both a bit quiet. Me, because I was thinking I would miss walking along with my new friend, but I think Vaisey was thinking about Jack. Or her hair. Or what larks she would have in the dorm.

I'm a bit jealous.

The trees were full of birds singing and you could

see the moors rising above Heckmondwhite. Some of the higher crags had bits of snow on the top still.

I hadn't really noticed how many birds sang in the woods, or the moors, probably because Vaisey and I didn't stop talking or acting things out as we walked along together. Or she was riding Black Beauty and I was revving my Harley. And doing wheelies.

Funny how quickly you get to be good friends with someone. I was going to miss trying not to alarm Black Beauty with my bike in the mornings.

When we reached Heckmondwhite, Vaisey scampered off. She yelled, "Got to dash because Bob is coming for me in his dude-mobile and I have to pack."

After my supper of "local" fish-and-chips from The Wetherby Whaler, it was nice to have Dibdobs around. She was by herself because Harold and the twins had gone to look at some cloud formations.

Dibdobs looked at me through her roundy glasses and said, "Tallulah, it's been so lovely having you here. The boys adore you, and so do I."

And she came and hugged me from the back, which made it a bit tricky because I was finishing my mushy peas. She said, "I just don't want to think about you not being here anymore."

That makes two of us.

I thought I would go and see Ruby.

Maybe the owls have hatched.

But there was no one around.

I tried calling her from the door of The Blind Pig. I didn't like to go in when she wasn't there. Partly because I was so shy about seeing Alex, but also because . . . oh dear. Mr. Barraclough was there. He was cleaning his pie-eating trophies in the bar.

I said, "I was just looking for Ruby."

He said, "She's up back, wi' Matilda."

I set off up the track behind The Blind Pig toward Blubberhouse, and before I saw her Matilda came hurtling down the track and crashed straight past me, because she couldn't stop her little bow legs.

Ruby shouted, "She couldn't stop a pig in a ginnel."

Whatever that means.

Ruby was hanging upside down from a low-lying branch.

You couldn't actually see her head, but you could see her knickers.

I said, "Hello, it's me. I can see your knickers."

She said from upside down, "I know, I've got my special apple catchers on."

I said, "I feel all miserable now because Vaisey has gone to stay at Dother Hall."

Ruby said, "I know, I miss her a bit, too. You should hang upside down, it doesn't half cheer you up."

"Does it?"

"Oh, aye."

I had my trousers on, so I thought I would give it a whirl.

As we hung there, I said to Ruby, "You're right, I do feel a bit better. I feel a lot redder, too."

She said, "Try swinging a bit at the same time. It makes you laugh."

Soon we were both giggling like upside-down loonies.

Ruby said, "Try swinging and putting your hands over your eyes at the same time. It's brilliant, you won't know which way up you are."

In for a penny, in for a pound.

She was right, swinging upside down with your hands over your eyes does make you not know which way up you are.

Ruby said, "What happened last night? Vaisey wunt tell me owt, but her hair looked like she'd bin electrocuted."

I said, "Actually the film was a bit like this. Lots of hanging around upside down."

Ruby said, "I'm not interested in the film. I'm interested in hanky-panky with boys."

It felt like being in a cosmic confessional. Just voices in the dark. Ruby threw a stick for Matilda upside down, but Matilda just watched it fly off past her. Then went back to trying to lick my face.

I said, "Well . . . it happened."

"Ooooooo."

"Yes. There was actual kissing."

Ruby's voice said, "What sort of kissing? Open-mouthed? How long for? Tongues?"

"Ruby, this a private thing."

"I know, I wunt to know the private thing, that is why I am hanging around waiting for you to tell me."

I went on.

"Jo did arm-around and snogging."

Ruby whistled. "With that Phil boy? The little cheeky one?"

I said, "Affirmative."

Ruby said, "I quite fancy him mysen."

"Ruby, you're only ten."

"I'm big for my age."

"OK, so you're a big ten-year-old. Phil's fifteen."

"I like older men."

"Stop being daft, Ruby, you barm pot."

"Shuffle over and say that to me face."

"I can't even see your face."

Ruby said, "Well, anyway, tell me what happened to you."

"Well, Jo got Phil, Vaisey got Jack, and I got this boy called Ben."

"Ben, what's he like when he's at home?"

"Well, he's quite tall and floppy."

Ruby said, "Good, good. Tall is good . . . floppy, well,

floppy can be all right, s'long as you don't mean he's a noddy niddy noddy."

"What?"

"You know, a bit simple in the noddle department."

Just then a male voice shouted, "Oy, you two, what the bloody hell are you doing?"

It was Mr. Barraclough. "I said this would happen, Ruby, if you mixed with the artists. The next thing you know I'll see you in the streets in Skipley with Matilda playing the piano whilst you pretend to stand very, very still."

Eventually he puffed off and we went back to sitting on the branch.

It was a lovely night with stuff tweeting, sheep scampering, cows frolicking. And then it got to be an even lovelier night because Alex turned up in his car. He got out and saw us up the hill on our branch and waved . . . and then started walking toward us.

I said to Ruby, "Is my hair all right?"

Ruby said, "Yes, a lot of folk like that matted look."

I tried to smooth it down casually, but my heart was thumping as Alex approached.

He is sooo good-looking, and he's smiling.

I hadn't seen him for ages.

Ruby said, "Shut your mouth, a bee might fly in it, and make a little bee house in there."

I tried to arrange my legs so that they looked less gan-gly.

Alex came and stood in front of us and crossed his arms.

"What are you two up to?"

Ruby said, "Lullah was telling me that last night she—"

I interrupted really quickly, "I . . . um . . . I was just going to tell Rube that I wanted to wrap the whole of Dother Hall in brown paper, as an, um, Art Statement."

They were both looking at me, not saying anything. So I burbled on.

"But there were only two pieces left, so I covered my book instead."

Alex said, "I can tell you're loving it, dahling, loving it at Dither Hall."

I said, "Well, yes I do. But I only came for a laugh really and now . . . now I . . ."

He looked at me right in the eyes and said, "Now you want to stay?"

I said, "Well, yes but—I couldn't do anything! Dr. Lightowler hates me because of my spontaneous legs."

Why was I telling him all this?

I just felt hypnotized when he looked in my eyes.

I mustn't start quacking or anything.

Alex looked at me again. Right in the eyes.

"Your eyes are the most amazing color, aren't they?"

Ruby said, "Oh no, now you've done it."

Alex suddenly pushed Ruby off the branch and she disappeared into the field. It really made me laugh, she looked so shocked. Alex grinned and then he did the same to me.

Pushed me off the branch!

As we were lying there in the field we could hear him go whistling off.

I looked at Ruby and said, "He, he pushed you, and then he pushed me. But didn't he say something about my eyes or something? What was it, I don't quite remember. . . ."

Ruby dusted herself down and pulled her apple catchers up.

She said, "Don't even think about it."

I did think about it, though. A lot.

Looking in the mirror in my squirrel room. He said I had "amazing" eyes.

Well, he said the color was amazing.

But that was as good, wasn't it?

I mean, why would you say "amazing" if you didn't mean it as good?

If you thought someone had really nonamazing eyes, you wouldn't mention it, would you?

Out of politeness.

You wouldn't say, "You've got the crappest eyes I've ever seen. Your eyes make me feel physically sick."

But on the other hand, say someone did have really crap eyes, you might distract them by mentioning a good feature to make up for it. Like their ears or something.

Maybe he was distracting me from my knees by mentioning my eyes.

Oh, I don't know.

And second of all he had pushed me off the branch.

Which in anyone's language is not what people do to grown-ups.

So . . .

And also what about Ben?

Even if I didn't want to go out with him, I wanted him to want to go out with me so that I could say sadly, "I'm afraid my heart is with another. I am wedded to Heathcliff, or Alex, as I know him."

That night as the owls hooted outside, I read about *Wuthering Heights* in my study notes about the Brontës. It said that Emily and Charlotte and Anne had to pretend to be blokes so that they could get their books published.

They had to display northern grit.

As I lay there with my squirrels and my budding corkies, I decided something.

I am going to display northern grit. Like the Brontë sisters. I'm not going to be put off by a bit of, "You're useless."

I bet they wouldn't be.

When Emily went in to her publisher and said, "I've written a book about some madman who lives on the moors. There's a lot of moaning and so on, and then the girl dies. I shall call it *Wuthering Heights*."

And they said, "Go home, love, and tell your sister not to come back with another story about a girl called Jane Eyre, because that will be rubbish as well. Get tha sen a little dog."

I wrote in my notebook:

I'm going to laugh in the face of fear, like the Brontë sisters.

"Just call me Fox. Blaise Fox."

I DREAMT ALL NIGHT that I was out on the moors like Cathy after she died. Trying to find Heathcliff. I was singing a special song: "I'm out on the moors, the wild moors." I'm going to write the lyrics in my notebook.

It took me ages to decide what to wear because you never know when you might bump into, um, someone's brother. We've got our first ballet class today so I need to have leggings and my special ballet shoes.

I am enjoying my special ballet shoes.

Looking at my special ballet shoes in their special ballet shoe box.

And I am enjoying them.

Special ballet shoes.

I put my special ballet shoes on. They feel good.

I feel like doing ballet!

I will improvise a ballet. I will think of being Cathy, flitting about in ballet shoes on the moors, lashed by cruel gales, looking for Alex—I mean, Heathcliff.

I sang from my notebook and danced, danced on the moors:

> *I'm out on the moors, the wild moors,*
> *Let's roll about in rockpools.*
> *Oh, it gets lonely without you,*
> *I hate you, I love you.*
> *It's Cathy, trying to get in your Windooooooow ow*
> *ow ow . . .*

There wouldn't be a bedside lamp on the moors. But if there was I bet I could find it with my shins.

It was funny not going to meet Vaisey.

Also, to be honest, it meant that I didn't have an excuse to hope that Alex was about. As I began to walk across the bridge and up the lane to Dother Hall, I was thinking, I bet they all had a pillow fight in the dorm last night and lashings and lashings of ginger beer. And as I was feeling a bit left out I saw Ruby skipping off to her mates. Yes, quite literally skipping. She saw me and shouted, "Oy, squeeze you later!!!"

It was like having a mad little sister. Which I've never had before.

And I had nice new friends.

And I had been kissed.

Also my corkers are on the move.

And I've still got the chance to do something to impress everyone at Dother Hall.

With my secret hidden talent.

That was secret.

And hidden.

Secretly.

It was a beautiful day, so I thought that I wouldn't wear my crash helmet on the imaginary Harley. I was riding along with the wind rushing through my hair, but then, nearly at the gates of Dother Hall, my lovely country drive was spoiled. I had to squeal to an imaginary halt because out of a bush jumped Vaisey, Jo, Flossie, and Honey.

Vaisey said, "Were you driving your imaginary Harley-Davidson?"

I nodded.

The ballet class was another low spot of embarrassment. When I tell you that the high spot was putting my special ballet shoes on, you'll get the picture.

Madame Frances hobbled in to her usual chair and adjusted her hot-water bottle. "Aaah. The ballet is the only true art. Before I had my accident I . . ."

I said to the girls under my breath as she rattled on

about her bad feet, "Is there anyone in this place who hasn't had an accident?"

This is the ballet.

We had to point our feet and go up and down. And then put our legs on bars, still pointing our feet, and go up and down. Then we had to hold each other's legs and go up and down. Pointing our feet. And then we did a bit more pointing and going up and down.

How can that be a good thing?

I said to Flossie, who had had to Sellotape her glasses to her head with all the pointy leg business, "When did this get invented? It's not proper dancing."

Flossie looked at me. "Lullah, I don't want to be unnecessarily rude, but I have seen your Irish dancing."

At the end we had to do jeté, which essentially means you leap up in the air with pointy feet.

Honey was really good at ballet. Really elegant and floaty. Even Flossie was good, although I think the Sello-taped glasses spoiled the total effect. Jo was good armwise but could only leap about an inch off the ground. When it was my turn, I was pleased because I went higher than everyone. I did it again and then noticed that Flossie and the others looked like they were having a fit.

Flossie said, "It's just that, it's just that . . ."

And then she started laughing uncontrollably.

I said, "It's just that what? I was leaping quite high."

Jo said, "I know, I know, the leaping is good—it's just

that when you leap you make a rabbit face."

Madame Frances was crying into her flask as we went out.

At break I pretended to go to the loo but went into the vegetable garden by myself.

The sun was glinting through the runner beans and Sidone's bicycle was leaning against the wall where all the plums were stored.

There was a watering can and a ballet dress in her basket.

Is that how she watered the garden? On a bike in a ballet dress?

Probably.

That's how arty she is.

I wonder what Cousin Georgia would do for the performance assessment if she were here.

I closed my eyes and tried to imagine her talking.

I could see her in my mind's eye, doing her disco inferno dance. And jiggling. Funnily enough she was wearing Sidone's tutu.

I think she was saying something like "Sugar Plum bikey"—but it was hard to tell because of the banana stuffed sideways into her mouth.

Despite a lot of protests from the girls, I am trying to get them to be in my bicycle ballet at the performance lunchtime. If I'm going to be on the course next term, I am going to have to pull out all the stops.

I said, "And the bicycle ballet might be a truly unforgettable event."

Jo said, "That is what we are all afraid of."

First I started with pleading. And saying I would get chucked off the course. And that they would never see my knees again.

Everyone looked at my knees.

I sensed they might be crumbling.

In the end they agreed that they would do the bicycle ballet.

Now all I have to do is to make up the bicycle ballet.

I'm going to go and make notes in my performance-art notebook.

The others wanted to know what it's about.

Aaah.

I said, "Well, the idea is that . . . not everyone is a ballet dancer . . . but that all life is art . . . and beauty can be found in the everyday . . . stuff."

They still looked a bit puzzled. They weren't alone.

Vaisey said, "Will there be singing in it?"

I said, "Yes, of course."

She got interested then.

"Will I be singing in it?"

"Oh yes."

"What will I be singing?"

Honey and Jo and Flossie all said, "Why can't we sing in it?"

I said, "You can—you're all singing in it!"

Vaisey said, "What are we singing?"

And I said, "Well . . . it's the Sugar Plum Fairy . . . theme song."

We're going to rehearse in secret every day. First we have to find some bikes.

But then fate took a hand in events at Dother Hall.

We were summoned to the Hall. There were candles burning and all the blinds were shut. Even though it was a spanking hot day. Then "Nessun Dorma" began playing, you know, that classical thing they had for the World Cup when even grown men cried.

The house lights were dimmed and Sidone Beaver came out onto the stage in a veil.

A full-length veil. She had something in her hands.

She was moving in a very odd way. Like she had a trolley for her feet.

Bejesus, she did have a trolley for her feet! She was sort of being drawn along on it to the center of the stage.

Then from underneath her veil Sidone spoke.

"I have here something . . . that says more than I could ever say in words about one of the finest artistes . . . it has been my privilege to work with."

And Sidone held up a pair of ballet shoes.

And that is the world-breaking news. Madame Frances has left and we have a new performance art dance tutor arriving today.

Afterward we were lolling about on the front steps outside, talking about Madame Frances leaving. I said, "Well, it's sad, of course, but look at it this way . . . Hurrrrahhhhh!!!"

We had been run-run-leaping for the best part of a fortnight.

Vaisey said, "What is she called, the new dance teacher? It was sort of like a James Bond name, wasn't it?"

I said, "Well, she can't be any odder than Madame Frances, I mean—"

At which point an old sports car came hurtling up the drive and stopped in front of us in a shower of gravel. A person dressed entirely in red plastic, with huge goggles, leapt out. She took off her goggles and underneath she had another smaller pair.

She said to us, "Just call me Fox. Blaise Fox."

The weird thing is that I immediately liked Ms. Fox. She is undeniably insane. We all agreed on that.

For our first session with her she walked around looking at us. She had a riding crop in her hand and she said, "I am looking at you and you are looking at me. This is very good. I am looking and I am liking. You are looking and you are thinking, 'I hope she doesn't hit me with her crop.' But that is because I am me and you are you. I am going to show you a film about the work I have done. Don't be frightened."

I have never seen anything like Ms. Fox's film.

There she was, dressed up as a German businessman on a train, sitting down with a newspaper, then she started slapping the commuters with her newspaper.

And then she was in a doggie outfit dancing around a kennel in a shopping center.

And finally, she was scratching her teeth in time to some music.

After we had watched the film, she said, "Right, you've got four minutes. Go find something in the studio and make up a little performance with it."

Wow.

And also wow.

And crikey Moses.

Everyone panicked and ran around the studio. I found an old bit of bandage backstage. I don't think it was used. I really hope it wasn't used.

I didn't really know what I was doing. I wrapped it around my hand leaving a little mouth hole. Like an Egyptian mummy. I think I was modeling it on the idiot boys without their "teef."

Before I had time to think, Ms. Fox blew a whistle and

shouted, "On the stage, let's see it. You!" And pointed to people.

Even Jo looked rattled. She'd found two drumsticks and put them in her hair and started to speak Japanese, I think.

Flossie put on a lampshade and started being a catwalk model.

Next it was Vaisey. She got up and said, "This is Vaisey." Then she put a curtain round her shoulders and said, "But this is Vaisey, star!" And burst into song: "Fame, I'm gonna live forever, I'm gonna learn how to fly. I'm gonna—"

Ms. Fox shouted, "Next!" And pointed at me.

I got up onstage and said, "Um, hello, Dad used to bring me stuff back from Egypt, and once he brought me a baby mummy."

Milly and Tilly started sniggering.

Then I said, "And here it is." And put my bandaged hand up.

Everyone was just looking at me. Like I'd gone mad.

I had.

I looked at the mummy. I said to it, "So you are an ancient Egyptian, then?"

I made the mummy nod its head and open and shut its mouth.

"That's very interesting." The mummy nodded.

I said, "You're very small for a mummy." And the

mummy started making muffled noises.

I said to it, "Well, there is no need for that kind of language. You are only letting yourself down, and ruining a lovely occasion."

The mummy made muffled noises again.

I said, "Right, that does it!"

And I wrestled my own hand to the floor and fought with it for a bit.

Some people clapped at the end.

Vaisey and Jo and Honey and Flossie stared at me.

As we were going out, Blaise said to me, "What's your name?"

I said, "Tallulah Casey."

She said, "Watching you is like watching someone whose pants are on fire. Strangely fascinating, keep it up."

I went home to write in my performance-art notebook. Already some of the slate is coming off the cover.

> Ms. Fox said "strangely fascinating." Is that good?
> Make the bicycle ballet "strangely fascinating."
> I've sort of mapped it out now.
> The girls sing the Sugar Plum Fairy song in chorus on bikes at the back.
> It starts with swirling snow as they go to the Land of Sugar and Sweets. (Note for swirling snow: Get a fan from Bob and lots of bits of paper.)

The chorus goes up and down the back of the stage on their bikes, first with legs out to the sides. (Will have to give big shove to get it across stage.)

Then one knee on the saddle.

Then both legs out at the back.

Then the Sugar Plum Fairy dance. I will be the Sugar Plum Fairy. (Costume note: Get lots of lollipops from village store and net underskirt from Ruby's ballet class.)

Could I get a unicycle from somewhere?

And dance with bike in center of stage before I ride off really fast, and then come gliding back on when I have momentum. With no hands.

Sucking two lollipops.

We've rounded up five bikes from Ruby, although one is a bit small as she had it when she was six. Jo can have that one. And the rest are ones that have been left at The Blind Pig after people had The Blind Pig special ale (Ruby says).

We've got the music. And most of the costumes, and we're rehearsing every day at the back of college.

I popped round to see the Rubster (and Matilda) on the way home, to see if the owlets were hatched yet and if Alex was about.

Ruby was eating an apple on the wall and she said she'd had a scientific idea.

181

"Dad is redecorating the downstairs ladies' loos, we could do your corker outline there. You know, a sideways outline. And see the difference the next time you are up here."

I said sadly, "Rubes, I don't think there is much chance of me being here next year. We've got our halfway assessments this week."

Matilda was hurling herself at my legs. She loves me. And goes mad with excitement every time she sees me. Ruby said, "Tha must smell like a doggie treat."

I said, casually, "Is Alex about?"

And Ruby tutted.

On Thursday, we were just going to check that the bicycles were oiled when I saw Alex in the corridor, talking to Lavinia.

I wished I had got my Barely Pink lipstick on to make me seem a bit more grown-up.

They looked like they were sharing a private joke, and Lavinia was grinning like a beaver.

As we passed them I was pretending to find something in my tote bag, but Lav spotted me and said, "Hellooo, little Oirish. I'm railly looking forward to your piece in the performance lunchtime. What is it called?"

Damn.

"Um, well, ah . . ."

She and Alex were looking at me.

"It's called . . . Dance of the Sugar Plum Bikey," I said wildly.

Alex had a slight grin on his face. He said, "Dance of the Sugar Plum Bikey. Yes, that's got a nice ring to it."

Lavinia smiled.

I smiled back.

But I didn't really mean it, to be honest.

And also she was the only person who called me "little" anything. I've never been called "little," even when I was little. Which was never.

Alex then said something that made my bottom quake a lot. "Look forward to seeing it, I'll be there at the performance lunchtime."

No!

Out in the bike shed, as we were oiling away, I said to the girls, "I can't do this!"

None of them said anything. They just went on oiling.

I said, "I want to stay on at Dother Hall, but I can't let Alex see my knees."

Flossie said, "You've got to do something, Lullah."

I said wildly, "I could do my Egyptian mummy thing!"

The girls handed me my bike.

Dance of the Sugar Plum Bikey

I THINK I HAVE sprained my ankle. Certainly I have destroyed a stoat mask made out of corn on the cob and a Hula-Hoop. The bike might be fixable.

It took Bob and a couple of the bigger girls a little while to untangle me from the stage lights. When I eventually hobbled back onstage for the crit there was a big round of applause. And I heard someone yell "Encore."

But I think they may have been being ironic.

The singing was good, the lights went on and off, the bicycles' chorus across the back was good, it was all going so well. I think the audience was a little bit surprised by my bike solo when I did a jeté and then the bike did a jeté but . . .

It was when I came to do my final pièce de résistance:

the lying on the saddle with my legs outstretched at the back. I was fine, I was balanced and focused. Vaisey's singing had reached a crescendo and I had my lollipops ready when my net skirt caught in the back wheel. And ripped off. Leaving me in my apple catchers.

In the spotlight.

The net skirt also jammed the wheel so the bike suddenly stopped and I plunged over the handlebars and into the backstage area through the blackout curtain.

Gudrun handed me a bin liner to cover my knickers. As I hobbled back in front of the audience, all I could think of was that maybe, by the grace of God, Alex had been in a minor car accident.

But then Lavinia hopped up onto the stage and said, "Well, that was soo railly good." And she glanced over to me. "And railly brave. Well done, you. You may have noticed that we have a tall, handsome stranger with us today. Besides you, Bob!"

Bob flicked what was left of his ponytail back. And gave a thumbs-up. He truly does think he is handsome.

Lavinia went on. "May I introduce you to the lovely Alex Barraclough. A local boy made good. Alex has starred in West End shows and is now on his way to take up a place at Liverpool Rep. So very exciting. He kindly said he would give us a word or two about today's performance. So over to Alex."

Alex stood up and swung himself onto the side of

the stage. All of the girls and most of the staff (especially Monty) were practically drooling and flicking their hair. Alex seemed very relaxed. He was probably used to it.

I pulled the bin liner around me more tightly. God, my ankle hurt. I could never ever go round to The Blind Pig again. I didn't want to listen to what he was about to say. And also I thought I was probably having a heart attack. My heart was thumping, my knees were bruised, and Alex had seen me in my knickers.

Vaisey was standing next to me and she squeezed my hand.

Jo mouthed, "You've got a lollipop in your hair."

Oh goodie.

Alex talked about "exploration" and "pushing boundaries" and not being afraid to fail. He said he'd enjoyed each piece in its own way.

Then as a final thing he said, "It's always hard to say what you like and why, but I have to say, in all honesty, I have never seen anything like the Sugar Plum Bikey. Never. It was ambitious and daring and . . . of course, accidents do happen. I once opened a door onstage and the whole set wall fell down. I haven't actually crashed off a bike headfirst into the wings. But maybe one day I will be lucky enough."

Everyone laughed.

I felt a bit better, actually. I think he was trying to

make me feel less of an idiot.

He went off to massive applause.

The girls were very nice to me. They said it was a brave effort and everything, but I knew.

We were getting our assessment marks after lunch. I couldn't eat anything so I sat on the front steps just looking at the moors. I didn't have what it took. I wasn't full of northern grit. I was full of some kind of grit from the stage floor, but it wasn't the kind I needed.

Blaise Fox came striding down the steps.

Please, please don't let her say anything horrid.

She said, "Tallulah, that was a triumph. You don't know how funny you are."

We got our assessments in little sealed envelopes. So this was it.

We went to our special tree to open them. I was hobbling along at the back.

Vaisey said, "Let's do it all at once. I'll count. Ready? One, two, three."

And we ripped open the envelopes.

Tallulah Casey
Dother Hall
Summer term assessment

Dear Tallulah,

You are clearly an intelligent girl as well as being very tall. You have an unusual presence and on the whole a slightly wild, but pleasing, disposition.

However, I regret that so far my staff and I have seen nothing that would suggest to us that you are cut out for an artistic career. As we have tried to emphasize, this is not a career choice for the fainthearted. In the time that you have left here, we hope that you will charge your glass with courage and show us that you can do something extraordinary.

Sidone

Your overall assessment is 45 percent

Vaisey, Jo, Honey, and Flossie all got over 60 percent.

Honey and Vaisey were specially mentioned for their singing.

I didn't want them to see my letter—but they wanted to.

Jo said, "Come on, Lullah, it can't be that bad."

I gave it to her and she said, "Blimey, that's bad."

Vaisey said, "She says that you're tall and you have an unusual presence. That's good, isn't it?"

And that's when little tears came splashing out of my eyes.

I didn't want to cry in front of them. But I was.

Vaisey started crying then as well, when she saw me.

She said, "Please don't, Lullah, I can't bear it if you cry and are upset. I think you are lovely, I thought you were lovely the minute I met you and you took me to Heckmondwhite High Street, which isn't there. But that is what I love about you."

Flossie and Jo put their arms around me. Jo looked up at me and said, "I bet you can do something, I just bet you can show them. What about singing a really big belting song that—"

Flossie said quietly, "The singing tutor sort of said that maybe, you know, Lullah should concentrate on other things."

Jo said, "Oh yes, yes, I remember. . . ."

No one could think of anything else to say. I was just standing in a huddle by our tree with my friends cuddling me. I've never been so unhappy and happy at the same time.

Then Jo said, "I know this is a bit of an odd thing to say, but it might show you that every cloud has a silver lining. When you were crying, I had my head accidentally on your corker area and I think you could even, maybe, get your first bra."

When I hobbled into the canteen at afternoon break, Lavinia was sitting with Dav and Noos. They waved when they saw me. I waved back, but then Lavinia did that "come over here" thing. I couldn't really pretend I hadn't seen them, so I had to go over.

Lavinia got up and gave me a big hug.

Why?

Have I turned into Huggy Bear since the bicycle ballet?

She was all sympathetic.

"How are you, little Oirish? You weren't bothered about the marks, were you? It's all so silly, railly, isn't it? I mean, even if you got ninety and a half percent, you can't go up to Andrew Lloyd Webber and say, 'Andrew, I got ninety and a half percent, give me a job, darling.'"

She went on. "I thought what Alex said was railly spot-on. You know, you did an experiment. OK, it went a teensy bit wrong, but you had the courage to do it. He was railly right. You know Alex a bit, don't you, Luls?"

Why was she calling me Luls? Where did that come from?

Lavinia was still in Alex world.

"I feel like I have known him for ages, and we have got so much in common. Is he around much?"

Oh, I see.

After break we trooped into Monty's class. It will be quite restful listening to him talk about himself, after what I've been through. In fact I feel quite fond of him. Now that I won't be seeing him again.

He bustled in and said, "Exciting news, girls, our next

project. Our next adventure. Takes us back in time. We're going to do a Mummers play."

At first I thought he said a mummy's play. And that everyone had been talking about me in the staff room.

Jo said, "Sir, what is a mummy's play?"

He said, "Mummers, dear, Mummers. I'm glad you asked that, Jo; it's very, very interesting."

Sadly, we now know that every time Monty says something is "very interesting" it is bound to be a story about him as a young man.

We were right.

Monty said, "I remember well the first Mummers play I was asked to do. It was a warm summer's evening in Chelsea. I had a lovely flat where I was wont to entertain friends after drama college. A way of us letting off steam. One of my friends, Simeon, was admiring my vegetables."

I looked at Vaisey and Jo. Where was this going to end?

Monty was still in Chelsea. "Why have roses when you can have fine, firm cauliflowers in your vases?"

Anyway, it turns out that a Mummers play is medieval.

Monty went on. "The 'Mummers' would dress up in motley (bits of old rag) with their faces painted blue and take sticks with sheep's bladders on the end of them to hit people with, and they would travel to local hostelries on a Saturday eve."

I whispered to Vaisey, "It sounds like The Blind Pig."

And she giggled and shook her hair about.

All afternoon we practiced the Mummers play. It's mostly fooling around and a bit of olde dialogue. Honey got to swan around singing as the maiden, Jo was St. George and belted people with her sword, and Flossie was the dragon. Vaisey was the wandering minstrel and Monty was the narrator. I didn't have anything to say because I was to be the horse.

Actually, to tell the truth it was spiffing.

We even improvised bits and I pretended to be Black Beauty, which made Vaisey laugh a lot. I seem to have lost a bit of my self-consciousness. I said that to the girls and Flossie said, "That's because you have no pride left."

She's not wrong.

At the end of the day, Monty said, "Now then, girls, I have a marvelous surprise. I thought we would pay a visit to The Blind Pig on Friday. And show them our little entertainment."

Oh no.

Crumbs.

Crikey.

And also, bejesus.

On Friday in Bob's Dude-mobile on the way to The Blind Pig, I said to Vaisey, "You should be the little horse. Tell

Monty, tell him, that you always are the horse. Remind him of your Black Beauty."

She said, "I can't now, it's too late. I'm the wandering minstrel and you don't want to sing, do you?"

I am someone who has got 45 percent for their talents and I am having to go into the lions' den, The Blind Pig. To give my 45 percent in front of a man who pretends I am a big lad. In tights. When Mr. Barraclough sees me as a horse, he will be so thrilled.

Well, I am not going to do it.

It's not just for me.

Matilda would never be able to hold her paws up in public again.

But as if in a horrific slow-motion nightmare, I found myself in the barn at the back of The Blind Pig. In a horse costume.

I tried to canter off down the road, but Dr. Lightowler spotted me and gave me one of her looks. So I pretended to eat some grass by the side of the road, as if I was getting into character, like Monty told us. I was pretending to *be* the horse. I tried to explain that to her, but she just shook her cloak and tutted.

All the Dother Hall staff had come along to support us. Blaise Fox was smoking a cheroot. She clicked her tongue at me and said, "Giddyup."

When we appeared in the main bar, Mr. Barraclough was beside himself with delight.

He was all dressed up and he had put a special bowler hat on the stag.

On the plus side, Ruby and Matilda were at dog obedience class.

Oh, it was bad. Worserer than anyone could have imagined. It had seemed good fun in the studio at Dother Hall. All "have at thee" and "jokes" that made no sense—"Hey diddly noddly noo, I will throw thee down the loo."

All I can say is that people in olden times must have had nothing to do. But no one else seemed to mind like I did. Honey was the maiden and swanned around singing with a lute. She was flirting with the village boys, who were like moths to a flame.

I said quietly to Vaisey, when I had done my horse dance, "If Alex or Charlie or Phil or even Ben turn up, please shoot me quickly or stab me to death with the stag's horns."

It was mostly the village lads watching and laughing. But I don't mean laughing in an entertained way, I mean in a "laughing at me" way. The Dobbinses were at the back of the crowd and the twins just looked and looked at me. Dibdobs clapped each time I did anything, even lean against the bench. And Harold joined in at one point and had an "amusing" fight with Flossie when he snatched her sheep's bladder and started hitting people with it.

Also, I was hot. My costume had legs hanging from it. And, besides a long tail, I had big ears and a mane.

The whole thing was awful, and I didn't understand why the rest of the girls thought it was so funny. Jo was bashing the big lads over the head with her inflated sheep's bladder like there was no tomorrow. She was shouting, "Have at thee, you varlant." And all sorts.

At last, it was the end and Monty came on as the narrator. There was a spontaneous round of applause. Just for his codpiece.

Monty was bowing and passing round his hat for change when one of the bigger lads grabbed Monty's codpiece. Oh, I wish I was kidding. And put it on his head like a bonnet.

Monty was delighted.

"Away you go, my boys!!! Play on, play on."

Then at a signal from Bob, who had been dressed as a jester with a drum, Monty strode into the center, his tights quite literally bulging with the strain of clinging to his stomach. He said:

"And now, good friends, forfend,

"And alack aday our tale is at an end,

"We hope we have in some small way,

"Added to this merry day.

"I thank you and alas must be away."

And he bowed and the whole of the back of his tights split.

I had to trot at the back of him until he could escape into the men's loos.

Afterward in the pub we were swigging ginger beer and eating crisps. Everyone was all excited and pepped up. Ms. Fox came to see us and said, "Well done. Well done. Brilliant interaction with the audience. Excellent use of sheep's bladders. Very, very good. And Tallulah, once again, a masterpiece in how to try and avoid being seen. I couldn't take my eyes off you. No one could."

Oh goodie.

Ruby was back and nagging me to come and see the owl eggs. She said, "I've got a feeling about 'em. . . . I think they're going to be popping out soon. What do you think we should name them?"

She said this to me, like I was the owlets' dad and she was the owlets' mum.

Ruby said, "It's really exciting, isn't it?"

I said, "It will be if Connie the killer mum is there."

Oh, I was so tired.

I tried to keep my end up, though, and be cheerful and nice, and join in.

About half an hour later, after a gallon of ginger beer and two tons of crisps, we were just coming away from the pub when the Hinchcliff boys swaggered up.

All three of them.

Ruben, Cain, and Seth.

It was like a standoff at the OK Corral.

And I was Trigger.

Why, oh, why hadn't I taken the horse costume off? I tried to tuck the dangly legs out of sight, but I still had a horse's body and tights on.

The boys just looked at us.

Then Ruben said, "Cor."

Jo and Vaisey and Honey were looking at them like mesmerized sheep.

And they were the wolves.

Ruby said, "Don't take any notice of 'em, it only meks 'em worse."

But I could tell the others were a bit fascinated.

The lads were sort of circling us. Seth and Ruben were dark, like Cain.

Then Seth pinched Honey's bottom. And she said, "Ouch, that weally hurt."

Seth said, getting really close to her, "Did it WEALLY hurt, love?"

Then Flossie pinched Seth's bottom and he leaped about a mile in the air.

He said, "Bloody hell, you're a strong dragon!"

Ruby said, "Clear off, you lot, otherwise I'm going to tell my dad about that chicken you stole."

Seth said, "You would an' all, you—"

But they began to slope off, making kissing noises. As Cain passed me he looked right into my eyes for a minute, just breathing and looking at me. From his dark eyes. And his dark-red mouth. From under his black hair. I felt like I was being drawn into a vortex of blackness. What did he want with me?

Then he said, "Look at the state of you."

He's like a wild animal

As we walked along Honey said, "They're vewy thexy in a no-good way."

I looked back to see Cain looking back at me. Then he did a clicking sound and one of the village girls, I think she's called Beverley, came out of the shadows. She got hold of Cain's arm.

Cain shouted out, "Night-night, girls, don't do nowt I wouldn't do." And he laughed.

Ruby said, "That Beverley has been forbidden ever to see Cain since the last time."

Vaisey said, "What happened?"

Ruby said, "Well, she was right keen on Cain and he, you know . . ."

We all went, "What???"

Ruby said, "Well, he snogged her and that, and then

she was all keen, and he gave her a ring and so she started telling folk they were engaged."

Vaisey said, "What happened then?"

Ruby said, "Beverley turned up at one of The Jones's gigs and Cain were with someone else."

Jo said, "What, she just turned up? He didn't say anything? What did she do?"

Ruby said, "She went down to the river and she threw herself in it."

We all went, "Oh my God."

Vaisey said, "Did she drown?"

And we all looked at her. Then she realized and went a bit red. She said, "What did happen?"

Ruby said, "Well, the river was only a few inches deep, so she sat down in it and ruined her frock, and that were abaht it. But she went to bed and wept for weeks, and that. Her dad were livid and started a family row with the Hinchcliffs, and she's not to speak to Cain again."

Cain is a bounder and a cad.

When we reached the Dobbinses' house, Jo, Flossie, Vaisey, and Honey decided to try, accidentally on purpose, to find the boys. They were going to have a look round to see if they were playing snooker in the village hall or having a game of football.

I said, "My legs are tired after all that trotting. I think I will hit the hay."

Flossie gave my head a little squeeze.

"That was very nearly a joke."

Ruby said to me, "What? What about the eggs?"

I said, "Maybe tomorrow."

She said, "Huh. I'll come with you lot, then."

Vaisey said kindly, "It's a bit late, Rubes, and I don't want your dad on my case."

So Ruby went grumbling off home to play with Matilda and her new squeaky bone. That Matilda is scared of.

As they left, Jo had one last go at persuading me.

"Ben or . . . Charlie might be there."

I was too fed up. I said, "No. I would love to, but I think I have pulled a fetlock."

I went into the Dobbinses' house. They were still out.

I sat in my squirrel room.

Looking at my horsie legs.

What a night.

I love my new friends, but they can do stuff. And they are not all weird and self-conscious like me. Like Vaisey. Even though her whole head was painted blue and she was charging about in bits of old rag, she enjoyed it. And Honey sang in a lovely voice, and Jo waggled her sword about and slapped the audience with it. And Flossie, well, Flossie was just Flossie. . . .

And Ben hasn't sent me a note or anything. Even though he did jabby-tongue business. That seems a bit rude.

201

I wish Matilda was here, trying to get up into my bed.

I may as well get in it myself. There's nothing else to do.

I even broke my rule about not being childish and put the squirrel slippers next to me. Because they were soft and furry.

I wrote in my performance-art notebook:

I feel all hot and restless.

I feel like there is some big mystery I don't know about.

Something, wild, rising up inside me.

Calling to me.

Maybe I've got a touch of the Wuthering Heights.

Out on the moors,

The lonely moors,

I roll around in sheep poo.

Heathcliff, it's youuuuu,

I hate you, I love you, tooooo.

Let me in, I'm here, it's meeeee,

Catheeeeeeee.

Look out of your windooooow.

I got up to look out the window toward Grimbottom. That could have been named for Heathcliff. Maybe I'll read the book Harold gave me, *Heathcliff: Saint or Sinner?*

Um. The first chapter is about him being an orphan.

Well, I'm practically an orphan, but I don't go round setting dogs on people and shouting. And being mean. In fact, Matilda likes me very much. I am a tall doggie treat to her.

Boys don't like me, though.

Ooooohhhhh. I can't concentrate on Heathcliff. I'm too hot and bothered. Where's the James Bond book that Dad gave me? Here it is.

Now where did I get to?

Oh yes. In Jamaica, it's the bit where Honeychile is so hot and the fans are going round and round in the hotel room. And the waves are crashing against the shore. And so Honeychile took off all her clothes and stood by the window. Yes, this is the good bit.

Bond went across to her and took a breast in each hand. But still she looked away from him out the window.

"Not now," she said in a low voice.

How does that work? Is that what you're supposed to do? Should I have said "not now" to Ben?

If I act it out, I might get an idea of what it feels like.

Although it's hard to imagine someone putting their hands over my corkers as I haven't really got any.

Maybe if I put socks down the front of my jimjams that would be more like corkers. Yes, but then I wouldn't know what it felt like to have a hand over each one.

Maybe, if I put the socks on my hands, that would give me more of an idea.

I'll use my big thick hiking ones.

OK.

Right, I am walking in a sexy way to the window. Phew, I am hot. I am imagining the Caribbean Sea crashing against the shed at the bottom of the garden. James Bond coming over to me. He is putting a hand over each breast. Oooh, the hiking socks are a bit prickly. I am looking away from him out of the window. I am saying, "Not now . . ."

Oh, dear Virgin Mary and all her cohort, there is someone down there looking up at me!!! I bobbed down beneath the windowsill.

The light was on in my room.

Had they seen me fondling myself with hiking socks??

I stayed absolutely still.

Perhaps they hadn't seen anything and were just looking at owls or . . .

A voice shouted up. "Have you gone all shy now? Why don't tha come out and play with me?"

And a girl's voice farther away said, "You think you're something."

And the boy said, "Correction, love, I KNOW I'm something. I'm Cain Hinchcliff."

★ ★ ★

When I was sure they had gone off I went and shut the window. For about twenty minutes, I lay on my bed. Those Hinchcliffs are not like anyone I've ever met before. Cain is wild. Not like a human being, more like an animal in trousers. It's like he gets pleasure from being bad. He'll probably make up a song about it, like poor Beverley.

Just then, something banged against my window.

Someone was throwing stones against it.

He was back.

Bloody Cain.

Well, I'm just in the mood for the big lairy lug. I've got nothing else to lose. He's seen me in my horsie legs and now, rubbing my corkers with hiking socks. What else can he do to me?

I went to the window and opened it and shouted down, "Where do you get your kicks . . . casualty?"

And Charlie said, "Er . . . no. I have come in friendship to worship the knees. Come down."

Gadzooks. I looked at myself in the mirror. Oh, what the bejesus could I do about myself?

Take my pajamas and the socks off, for one thing. I did that and I put my jeans and a T-shirt on. And shook my hair about.

When I opened the front door, Charlie was slouching against the garden gate. He looked really cool. He's lovely-looking. And I realized how glad I was to see him again. It had been a bit awkward last time, thinking about why he didn't come to the cinema. But he must like me as a friend if he has specially come round to see me. So I beamed at him. And he did a megagrin back.

He said, "You've covered the knees and I specially came to see them. Can I just feel one? To get the impression of knee."

He was making me laugh.

I said, "OK. Just a quick feel, though."

He said, "Bend your leg up, like you are a horsie standing on one leg."

I said, "They told you, didn't they?"

He said, "Who? What? Oh yeah, go on then, they did tell me. They're over by the bus stop wagging about. Show me your horse costume."

"No."

"Well, describe Sugar Plum Bikey to me then."

I was outraged.

"They have broken the rule of—"

Charlie said, "The Tree Sisters?"

"Yes, yes, the Tree Sisters' rule."

Charlie reached down and touched my knee.

I said, "Ouch."

He said, "Whoaaa, that's better. I can feel myself full of a strange energy. I normally only get it when the headmaster sees me win the six-mile run and he knows that I haven't been in it."

I suddenly felt a bit shy. I don't know why. I mean, Charlie and I were friends, he'd made that clear, hadn't he? So I should just be friendly.

But I've never had a boy who was a friend before. What is friendly? Oh, I know.

"Do you want to see some owl eggs?"

He looked at me.

"Do I want to see some owl eggs?? Do I want to see some owl eggs?"

I was looking at him.

He was going on. "Who wouldn't want to see some owl eggs?"

I said, "Come on, then, they are down here."

He said, "Tallulah, the answer to who wouldn't want to see some owl eggs is . . . me!!!!"

I said, "Really?"

And he looked at me.

"You're serious, aren't you, you are genuinely thrilled that you have found some owl eggs?"

I nodded. I felt really stupid now.

And he smiled.

"Come on, then, you crazy-kneed girl."

And we set off down the track to find the eggs.

When we went into the barn, the door creaked back. And in the gloom we could see a glow of whiteness. The eggs were lying there, all white and weird. They looked like they were a bit cracked. I hope Connie hadn't sat on them too hard. I also hoped she wasn't around anywhere. It was quite spooky in the barn and a whistling wind blew up from nowhere.

Charlie said, "Yes, they are definitely eggs."

I could hardly see his face in the dark of the barn.

What a night I had had: Mummers play, corker rubbing, and now Charlie turning up and me bringing him to look at eggs.

I said, "It's a bit odd, isn't it? Me and the knees, and showing you the eggs. I'm sorry I'm so odd and . . . odd."

Charlie said, "You're not odd. . . . You're great, I think."

And he sounded like he meant it.

I could hardly believe it.

I've never had anyone, well, a boy person, say that to me before.

I felt like singing my little song. But I know now to resist the call of "Hiddly diddly diddle."

Charlie came nearer to me.

"Lullah, things can be quite, erm . . . complicated in life, can't they? You know, it's not just you."

Just then there was the most horrible screech, and something swooped low and brushed against my face. I was so shocked, I actually grabbed Charlie. Like in a really crap film.

Oh, it was so scary. In fact, it was Connie. Come to

208

check on her eggs. I could hear her chuntering and screeching up in the eaves of the barn.

And suddenly I burst into tears.

Everything in my body seemed to just dissolve into
tears.

Charlie said, "It's all right, Lullah, it's not going to
hurt you. It's just checking on the eggs. Come on." And he
got hold of my hand and took me outside.

He looked so kind and caring in the moonlight, and
sort of handsome and brave.

Like Mr. Darcy.

Maybe he would pick me up and carry me home. In
his breeches.

And for a second, he just looked at me. Then he put
his hand under my chin. And stroked my cheek with his
other hand.

Cheek stroking! Did that come before snogging? Oh
my God. Was this my second kiss???

But he didn't kiss me. He said, "If I'd known that you
were going to the cinema, I might have come. And that
would have been stupid."

What did that mean?

And then he looked at his watch and said, "Come on,
otherwise I get the usual thrashing from the headmaster,
if I'm late."

As we walked along, I felt shaky and strange.

To fill in the gaps I said, "I don't think you are allowed

to beat schoolkids anymore, it's against the Geneva Convention and European Euro thing."

He laughed and said, "Lullah, you've not seen our headmaster. I am taller than he is. And I've got more legs."

More legs?

When we got to the Dobbinses' gate, he gave my arm a little squeeze and said, "See you soon." And he went off into the night.

I was just going through the gate when he came back again.

"Lullah, I . . ."

I didn't know what to say. I said, "Oh."

He said, "Yep."

I said, "OK, well, good."

And we looked at each other, and then he said, "Night, night."

What did that mean?

I woke up dreaming about Mrs. Rochester cantering around my bedroom and then realized that the horsie legs were draped over the end of my squirrel bed.

I had my breakfast and sat on the wall, waiting for Ruby to come out of The Blind Pig. I am not keen to go in there after last night and the Mummers play. Already, one of the regular lads in the darts team has passed me by, neighing. Uh-oh, Mr. Barraclough has seen me. He will have a field day.

He said, "Ay up, I'll just go get thee an apple, my beauty. Now don't you poo on my front path."

Oh, this is appalling.

Ruby came skipping out like a whirlwind with Matilda. When she saw me, she started jumping up and down.

"They're here, they're here! The owlets. Hooray! Hooray! Say 'hooray,' Matilda. Say 'hooray,' like I taught thee at obedience class."

Matilda lay on her back and looked up at me with her lovely buggy eyes. She put her legs in the air.

I said, "Is that hooray?"

Ruby said, "Aye, she's so excited, she's had to have a bit of a lie down."

I gave Matilda a big scratch on her tummy and she quivered like a jelly dog.

Ruby was chatting on. "I've called them Ruby and Lullah. Do you like the names? One of them is bigger than the other and it's got reet long gangly legs, so I thought that one should be thee."

I laughed at her, but I'm secretly loving it that she called the owlets after me and her.

We went down the back way to the barn and opened the door really carefully, shielding ourselves from Connie, in case we needed to.

Ruby said, "We'll just peep in and scarper. That was what I did this morning."

I yelled, "Yarrooooo!" But nothing happened. So we

went over to the corner where the eggs were, but they weren't eggs anymore, they were living, breathing owlets!!!!

Oh, I love them.

Ruby picked one of them up gently and said, "Do you see what I mean about Lullah's legs?"

I said, "Yes."

I felt a big surge of love for little Lullah. She was cheeping and blind and had gangly legs. I said to Ruby, "I am going to become like a big sister to them and always look out for them, and defend them against . . ."

Ruby said, "Right big mice?"

She was grinning through her gap teeth. Then she held little Ruby down for Matilda to sniff. Little Ruby cheeped and Matilda nearly fell over backward, and raced for the door.

I started laughing, but then I said, "Maybe Matilda has used her dog hearing, and knows that Connie is coming back."

Ruby started to say, "Dog hearing? I got in her dog basket once when she was snoozing and she didn't even—" Then something creaked, and we shoved the owlets back in the nest and legged it for the door.

As we jogged away from the barn, Ruby said, "Any more lad stuff? Did the lasses track down the Woolfe lads?"

I said, "Yes, but something funny happened to me when I went home. I was—"

And I was just about to tell her about the Charlie incident when Ruben came strolling by with his pigs.

Ruben winked and said, "Ay up, Rube."

And she said, "Ay up, Rube."

And we both laughed.

It was water off a duck's back to Ruben. He said, "Either of you fancy a snog, as I'm doing nowt?"

Ruby said, "Yeah, that would be great, wouldn't it, Tallulah?"

Pardon?

Ruben said, "Really?"

And Ruby said, "Oh, look, there's a pig, can you see it, up there in the sky?"

As he sloped off, clicking his fingers, she said, "All of the Hinchcliffs have been like that since they were about two."

At which point we noticed Cain, sitting on a gate sucking on a piece of grass.

Ruby said, "What's he up to?"

I said quickly, "Why don't we have a proper run for a bit?"

Too late. Cain saw us and shouted over, "All right, girls? Going to play with tha dollies? Or have tha got something else to play with?"

I do officially hate him.

I turned my back on him and started walking on. I heard a girl's voice say, "Cain, where's tha been?"

Then Ruby said, "Oh my God, this time he's done it."

I looked round and he was snogging a girl. What was news about that?

I said to Ruby, "That Beverley girl wants her head testing."

Ruby said, "It's not Beverley."

And it wasn't.

Ruby said, "It's Seth's girlfriend."

Heathcliff, it's me

WHEN I GOT TO Dother Hall, I felt like a month had gone by, so much had happened. It was really only two days since I had seen the girls, but I had been through the wringer of life. I wouldn't know where to start to tell them everything.

Was I going to tell them everything?

As I reached the gates, Vaisey came hurtling out to hug me, her hair shaking and shimmying about. She said, "Lullah, guess what? Phil told me that Jack thinks I'm cute!!!! Cute!!!"

I said, "Gosh. And goodie. That's goodie. And spiffing and everything."

Vaisey said, "I know, I know. AND Jack is going to be coming here on Friday . . . because . . . The Jones have asked him to be their new drummer!"

Oh goodie, The Jones will be around on Friday.

★ ★ ★

I didn't have any time to talk to the girls about my news because we had mime with Monty, first thing. He was so excited about it that he came and got us ten minutes early. Hustling us into the small studio, he loosened his bow tie and said, "Today we are going to learn how to express ourselves, but not through voice. Let's begin. I will go first."

He put on a sailor's hat and started to sway from side to side.

Then he put a hand over his eye, like he was looking into the distance.

Then he looked sad.

Then he looked into the distance again.

And jumped up and down, looking pleased.

He fell to his knees, putting his hands in prayer position. Then leapt up again and did a war dance.

At the end, he said, "So, girls, what happened?"

Flossie said, "Were you a drunken sailor?"

Monty looked a bit annoyed.

We knew it was some sort of sailor because of the hat, but then Flossie said, "Well, were you on a cross-Channel ferry in a storm?"

Monty got exasperated and told us that he was Columbus discovering America.

I don't know how we were supposed to know that.

I said to Vaisey, "Wasn't Columbus Spanish or something? He should have done a little flamenco dance

216

instead of just the swaying."

At that point Ms. Fox came in and said, "Hello, carry on as if I am not here."

Then she lay down on the floor.

Monty said, "Now, ladies, it is your turn. Think yourself into whatever it is you are portraying. Be the thing or person inside."

We had to get into groups of three and be at a party. The person who was "being" whatever they were being, had to convey to the other two by their actions what they were "being."

I felt strangely calm for once.

I went and crouched on a chair.

I was "being" Connie.

Like Monty had told us, I thought about the "qualities" of owliness. My wise nature. Where my home might be. What I would have for supper. Mouse, I fancied. I began to only really think in hoots. I thought about my bottom being comfortable on a tree. And what I would do if I wanted a pee. I looked around to see how far I could twist my head. And how long I could stare.

No one came near, although Flossie did offer me a mime cheesy wotsit (I think). Then she and Vaisey went back to pretend conversation and mime snack-eating.

Eventually I started waving my pretend wing.

Flossie came up, dabbing at the floor, like I had spilled my pretend drink.

This was hopeless.

I caught Vaisey's eye and raised my lower eyelids slowly. Surely, that would do it.

It didn't.

So then I laid an egg.

People can be very thick even when offered the best of mimes. Flossie said, "Are you having a poo?"

Monty said, "I think we will leave it there."

Then everyone had to guess what had gone on.

How on earth could anyone have thought that I was sitting on a space hopper at a party?

What fool would do that?

Monty said, "So what was the mime all about? You seemed somehow disturbed and angry. Was there some inner conflict expressed in your performance?"

I said, "Yes, there was, sir, I was an owl laying an egg and . . ."

Everyone fell about laughing, literally in Flossie's case. . . . They were all begging me to do it again.

I hadn't meant it to be funny.

I was really trying to be an owl.

As we went out Blaise Fox said, "Come with me to the roof, Tallulah."

Was I so bad that she was going to push me off?

We went up the winding stairs to the dorm, and then up some tiny narrow stone steps that led to the roof.

I had never been up to Mrs. Rochester land. You could walk along on the flat bits between the towering chimneys, and there was a parapet that went all the way round. And huge gargoyles on every corner of the roof. Blaise led the way and we went to lean on the stone balcony.

You could see for miles over the woods and moors, all the way to Grimbottom. There was a building to the left, beyond the woods, that looked a bit like Dother Hall. . . . Ooh, that must be where Phil and Charlie and Jack were. The mysterious Woolfe Academy.

Ms. Fox said, "Do you want to stay here, Tallulah Casey?"

I thought at first she meant "did I want to stay on the roof," but then I realized she meant at Dother Hall.

So I said, "Well. At first I just came here so I didn't have to go camping with my brother. And eat butterfly sandwiches."

Ms. Fox said, "Butterfly sandwiches. Go on. . . ."

So I went on, "But now I sort of . . . well, love it here. I want to . . . you know, *do* something good."

Ms. Fox lit a cheroot. But to be fair to her, there wasn't a "strictly no smoking" sign on the roof.

I struggled on, "But you know, you've seen me, the bicycle thing . . . my horsie. The owl. It's not enough to just think you want to do something, is it? You have to be able to do it."

She said, "And do you know what I think you can do?"

I said, "Be an idiot?"

She smiled at me. "But I believe you have a special quality."

Blimey.

She went on. "It's a mix of energy and, I think . . . a talent for comedy."

Yippee. Maybe.

Blaise looked at me and said, "I've been thinking about our end-of-summer-school *Wuthering Heights*. It's going to be a musical. And I want you to be the lead."

Crumbs.

Me?

Cathy?

I had the hair for it—I could swish it about. And I could sing my song:

I'm out on the moors, the windy moors,
Let's roll about in mud pools,
Or sheep poo, I hate you, I love you, tooooo.
Heathcliff, it's me, tap-tapping on your windooooow.

Then I came out of my made-up world.

Wuthering Heights, the musical.

I said, "Um, the only thing is, I can't sing."

And she said, "I know, it's a comedy version. And I want you to be Heathcliff."

★ ★ ★

When I got back to Heckmondwhite, the whole village was in a state of high excitement as there is going to be a mass skipathon at nine o'clock with tuba playing and the skipping rope is finished. And the village shop is staying open half an hour later, just in case someone needs a bag of humbugs.

I had walked home from Dother Hall in a dream. I was so shocked that I didn't tell the girls what had happened in Mrs. Rochester land, I told them I was rushing off to see the owlets. They wanted to come and see them too, but they all had singing lessons.

As I tramped along the woodland path, I was confused.

What does Ms. Fox mean, she wants me to play Heathcliff?

He's a boy.

Does she mean I am like a boy?

I tried to ask her, but she said I have to figure it out for myself and to come back to her with my ideas, about how to "be" Heathcliff.

And to not feel sorry for myself because it is unattractive in a girl with my knees.

The Dobbinses were leaving the house as I got there, taking sandwiches for the skipping participants. Dibdobs gave me a big hug as she left.

She said, "Oooooohhhhhhhhhh."

And the twins hugged my knees and went, "Ooooohhh, sjuuuge."

They are wearing beanie hats. Which I think is a bit cruel of Dibdobs.

Beanie hats on bowl-headed boys.

I went up to my room to think about the *Wuthering Heights* thing.

And to make notes in my performance-art notebook.

I spent about an hour on it.

It reads:

Breeches and a mustache.

I thought I would pop along to see the owlets again. It would take my mind off the Heathcliff thing. I was going to make bloody sure Connie wasn't anywhere around, though. And by the way, where was the owl dad, when he was needed?

When I carefully went into the dark barn the owlets must have sensed I was there because they started cheeping and peeping. I went over to the nest. Oooooohhh, they are cute and fluffy. Still blindy, though. They were opening and closing their beaks, but I didn't have any owl snacks for them. Ruby might know what they like.

I said softly, really close to their ears . . . Do they have ears?

Anyway, I said near to where ears would be if they had

them, "It's me, big Tallulah. And you are little Tallulah and little Ruby. I am not as furry as you but my eyes are quite big. And when you can open yours, that is what you will see. I love you, little owls."

I stayed for a while, chirping with them. I did touch their little heads but then I thought that Connie might be able to track me down by my smell. And that made me think it was spooky and dark in the barn, so I thought I would go.

As I came out of the barn, I saw Cain with his arm around Beverley.

Cain, AGAIN.

I am haunted by him.

Shouldn't he have a job, tupping sheep or whatever they do on the moors? Striding about with a big black surly dog, like him.

Oh, actually, he has got a dog.

A big black surly dog. Growly and black. It came bounding up to me and leapt up, and put both its huge paws on my chest. Ow.

Cain said, "Oy, dog. Get down. Mind your manners with the young miss. Nivver just jump up on a lady, you must always give her face a quick lick first."

The dog got down and went behind Cain.

And he and Beverley laughed.

Oh, great balls of fire, I hoped she wasn't with Cain when I had been doing the corkers rubbing. She was looking at me like she didn't like me.

He was looking at me as well. He's got incredibly long black eyelashes, like a girl's.

He does a lot of looking.

Up and down he looked.

It was making me nervous, so I said, "What's the dog called?"

And he said, "Dog." Typical.

Thank Angel Gabriel and all his cohort, because Ruby came skipping along with Matilda. My two little pals.

Cain's dog looked at Matilda.

Blimey, there was probably going to be a dogfight now. Dog growled. And Matilda lay on her back and put her legs in the air. She was doing "hooray."

Cain laughed and said, "Bloody women."

Cain is just like Heathcliff.

Then he said, "Come on, Dog." And he started walking off.

Beverley said, "Aren't tha gonna walk me back fust?"

And he said, "Does it look like it?"

Ruby tutted and went into the barn, to say good night to Tallulah and Ruby.

Beverley looked a bit sad and I didn't know what to say.

When Ruby came back, Beverley said to her, "He's a right pig, that Cain."

Ruby said, "I know; why don't tha know?"

And she said, "I dunt know, I just think that if he got tha right sort of girl, he'd happen be happy. See thee at skipping." And she went off ahead of us.

On our way back, Rubes and I popped to the skipathon on the village green.

The villagers were lining up to skip with a fourteen-foot skipping rope.

Harold was holding one end. He had the Christian Table Tennis team hanging on to him. And Dibdobs was on the other end, and she had the whole of the Brownie pack holding her waist.

Two lines of people queued up to skip.

The aim was to get the whole village skipping at once.

I should have told the girls to come, it was hilarious. I was a bit worried that the Hinchcliffs might be there, but Rubes said they don't join in with village stuff.

Back in my bed, I've written this in my performance-art notebook:

They are the dark outsiders.
Up on the moors.
The Wuthering moors.
Planning their dark deeds.
In their dark farm.
Ruben, Seth, and Heathcliff.
Hmmmmmmmmmmm.

It's nearly midnight, but I can hear laughing and yelling from the green, people are carrying on skipping, and the

Dobbinses are still out. I wonder if they have ever stayed up till midnight before?

The next morning when I got to Dother Hall, Vaisey came dashing out again to see me. I thought that Vaisey had hit her peak yesterday, but today she is on cloud nine. And her hair is on cloud ten. I've never seen it look so perky.

She's got a little note. From Jack.

She was so excited and red and said, "He must have delivered it in the night. It was in my postbox this morning."

How romantic, to have a note delivered to you.

I said, "What did it say?"

Vaisey was all pink and her hair was dancing about.

"It was really nice."

I said, "But what did it say!!!"

"He's been busy with The Jones and he says he'll be here on Friday, and will see me then."

Wooohooo. Vaisey's first date!!

This afternoon we "brainstormed" the *Wuthering Heights* production with Ms. Fox. And she announced to everyone that I was going to be Heathcliff and that Vaisey is Cathy. We are going to improvise toward a production. It's going to be about wildness and youth and passion. With music.

Ms. Fox said, "Let's start now. I want you to 'go wild,' in whatever way you like. I'm going to put 'The Ride of the Valkyries' on, so just let yourselves go. Find your inner gorilla."

So we crashed around the studio, fighting and running and shaking everything to music. It was really good fun.

Then we had to do "contained violence and anger." To the "1812 Overture."

Flossie was very good at it. And Jo had to be hauled off one of the lighting stands.

Then we had to lose our tempers in a foreign language.

I tried Norwegian because of my mum. And was able to use "Sled-werk" in a sentence:

"*Du grossen biggen Sled-werk nit.*"

I haven't laughed so much for ages.

Ms. Fox was falling about.

We went and sat under our tree at lunchtime. Even though it did look like there was a storm brewing.

Everyone was jabbering on about *Wuthering Heights.* Ms. Fox has got us all talking ideas. Flossie and Honey are the wind-singers. And the heavenly chorus. And Jo is thunder and lightning. She's got loads of drums to bang and a wrestling match with one of the village folk, so she is made up.

The whole thing is an all-singing, all-dancing extravaganza.

It's going to be filmed.

For posterity.

227

With me as a boy.

In a mustache.

I said, "Why are none of you surprised that I am Heathcliff?"

Jo said, "Well, you did the owl, and that was good."

I said, "You thought I was a space hopper."

Vaisey said, "Well, what about your horsie thing? I liked that."

And Flossie said, "You've got your own mustache."

Ms. Fox said she thinks my Irish dancing should be the finale. I started to say something about, where did that fit into *Wuthering Heights*, I don't remember Heathcliff (or Cathy) being Irish, but no one was paying attention. Vaisey wanted to talk about what she should wear on Friday. And also how to keep her hair under control.

I said, "Don't any of you think it's a bit out of the blue?"

They looked at me.

I went on. "Choosing me for the lead role. Don't you think that's odd?"

Flossie said, "Ms. Fox says it was inspired by your bicycle ballet performance. But without the bicycle or you crashing into the wings."

Harold and Dibdobs are very interested in my portrayal of Heathcliff.

Harold went on a lot about his inner "female." He said, "It is something we explore a lot at our Iron Man camps.

This is a really very interesting topic. In fact, I have a book that we were reading round the campfire that I must rootle out for you. We used to dress the twins in dresses until they started playschool."

I didn't know what to say. Except, "Golly."

The book that Harold gave me is called, *A Real Man's Guide to Soft Goods: How to Knit Your Own Socks.*

Why was he so interested in socks? What did he know? Had Cain spread the word around the village?

On Thursday, after I had accidentally stepped through an imaginary wall into the fireplace in her French play, Dr. Lightowler said to me, "Have you thought about what you will do in show business when you leave here, Tallulah? Perhaps the box office? Or theater cloakroom attendant?"

She hates me.

"Get your ears on, dudes!"

PRACTICALLY THE WHOLE COLLEGE was hanging around the sound studio at lunchtime. The Jones were supposed to have come in this morning, and Bob was fretting around. He had a T-shirt on with a teacup on the front of it. It said underneath, *I'm the mug with the band*.

On the back it said, *Duh*.

We could hear him in the sound studio, going "One two one two . . . Let's hit it, lads!!!!!" And then smashing the drums and cymbals like a madman.

It was a really hot day. Even Gudrun had let her bun down. Bumblebees were dozily bonking about, and that is when The Jones drove up the driveway. On a tractor.

When the rest of the girls heard the tractor they rushed out screaming, and I nearly choked on my banana. Seth was driving and Ruben and Cain were standing on the running board. All of them dressed in black. They got down from the tractor with their guitars and looked as if they always had sixty girls gawping at them.

Honey said, "Vewy cool."

As Seth went in, he looked at Flossie, and winked and said, "Oh yes."

Flossie took off her glasses, tossed her hair, and said, "Hi, y'all," in her Texan accent.

Cain came last, walking really slowly up the steps. He looked at the "Absolutely No Smoking" sign.

He got a cigarette out and lit it. He let the smoke curl out of his lips.

Oh crumbs.

He was smoking in a "no smoking" area. He was smoking by the "Absolutely No Smoking" sign.

He took a drag, and then he stubbed it out on the sign!

He said in his deep dark voice, "I dunt even smoke, but I do what I want, when I want. Because I am The Jones."

And he pushed through the crowd, who backed away from him.

I rolled my eyes at the girls.

"'I AM The Jones'? What he should have said is 'I AM the prat.'"

Jo said, "He is bloody good-looking, though, isn't he?"

And then coming up the driveway, we saw Jack. Vaisey went bright red to match her hair.

He was a bit red-faced himself and carrying a cymbally

thing. He said "Hello" when he saw us, and stopped.

Vaisey seemed to have lost the power of speech, so I said, "All right, Jack? What are you doing here?"

And he said to me, although I could tell he was looking at Vaisey, "I've come to play percussion for The Jones, I'm, you know, maybe going to be in the band, or something."

We were doing enthusiastic backup nodding and trying to get behind Vaisey at the same time.

Jack said, "Yeah, well, I've got to do a lot of catching up because there's a gig next week and . . . but . . . anyway, are you all right, Vaisey?"

Vaisey looked like a startled earwig. "Yeah, I, er, I got sixty-five percent for my singing. . . ."

He looked genuinely pleased.

"Great, that's great. . . . I meant to, you know, after the, erm, vampire bats, I was going . . ."

Then Cain appeared back at the top of the steps.

Jack sort of hesitated for a minute, and then said, "Er, I'd better go in . . . I . . . er . . . See you later."

And he did a little wave to Vaisey. And went after Cain.

Vaisey has been driving us mad all afternoon. Talking about Jack.

At one point, Bob popped his head round the door and said, "Get your ears on. The Jones will be live at five. In the main theater. Rock and roll!!!"

I was certainly not going to go.

Cain might already have written a song about me: "She's Got Those Corker-Rubbing Blues."

But on the other hand I could stand at the back, where he couldn't see me.

And crouch down a bit.

And look at him.

And see what he did.

Vaisey has been up to the dorm about eight times and come down in something different every time. We crowded into the theater after college. All the students were there, and the teachers.

It was like going to a proper gig.

Probably.

Sidone had got dressed up in pedal pushers and a Lurex top. She was already practicing doing the jive with Monty.

Jo said, "That is one of the oddest things I have ever seen."

I decided I am going to really observe Cain and base my Heathcliff on him.

There was still no sign of them at quarter to six. We could hear shouting going on in the passage. Not excited shouting, more like "having a barney" shouting.

The lights went up onstage and Jack went to sit at his drum kit. Vaisey applauded like mad. Then went bright red.

Then Seth came on with his guitar. He didn't even

look at us, he just started tuning up. Flossie wolf whistled. The girls oohed and aaahed.

Then Ruben came on. And they oohed and aaahed again.

Five minutes went by, and eventually Cain came on.

And just stood there. In black. Moody and black and dangerous.

There was silence as Cain looked out into the audience. He shook his head, like he'd seen a bunch of idiots, and said into the microphone, "This one is called, 'Is It So Very Wrong to Want You Dead.'"

And they played. And Cain sang.

Well, to tell you the truth, he didn't sing. It was more sort of growling and snarling and moaning down the microphone, whilst the band behind him made a whirlwind of noise. Jack was thumping away at the drums.

Then they played their next one, called "Shut Up, Mardy Bum." Followed by the classic, "Girlfriend in the River, I Know, I Know It's Really Serious."

It was the weirdest, most gothic gig I have ever been to. Even though I have never been to a gig.

Sidone and Monty tried to jive but gave up and just moved their shoulders around.

Cain was like an animal in pain. And he seemed really angry. With everything. He hit the microphone. He kicked the stand. He pointed at people. He even kicked Bob's special speaker with "Wizard" written on it. Bob went and stood by it with a broom.

At the end, Cain came forward and said huskily, "That's it, leave us alone."

The girls went mad for them.

Amazing.

Then, as Cain was storming off, he said something to Seth.

And Seth got hold of him and belted him.

Then Cain hit Seth and said something else.

Then Ruben came across and tried to break them up, and he got hit.

And then they all went off, fighting.

Amazing.

As we stood there, being amazed, Jack was left sitting behind his drums. He looked offstage for a second and then started dismantling his kit.

Vaisey said, "Should I go over?"

And we all went, "Yeah."

So off she toddled and got up on the stage. Jack smiled when he saw her. A bit shyly, but then they were chatting and he was letting her hit his cymbal. Thank goodness, and also, Yaroooo!!!

The Hinchcliffs came swaggering back, led by Cain, who had a bleeding lip. I bobbed down behind Flossie. They were signing autographs and also letting girls write their phone numbers on their arms. How ridiculous.

When they were ready to go, Cain looked up and saw Jack and Vaisey talking and laughing, and shouted over, "Jack, we're out of here."

Vaisey looked at Jack.

And Jack looked at Cain.

And then he looked down and started packing his kit up really quickly.

Vaisey stood there like a little red lemon for a minute or two, and then disappeared out of the stage door.

An hour later we found her up on the roof looking out to Grimbottom. And crying.

She must have been crying for an hour because her eyes are all tiny.

And her hair is droopy.

She wouldn't come in, so in the end I headed home and the others took her a blanket.

Back in my squirrel room, I decided I am definitely going to make our *Wuthering Heights* production about Cain.

I've been practicing in the mirror. I put my hair back in a ponytail, and I can do his harsh looks now.

There are some illustrations in the book I've got, and Heathcliff has got a white shirt on with a long black jacket. And riding boots. And a mustache.

I hope Cousin Georgia won't mind, but I've trimmed her mustache. It had droopy curly ends on it that made me look a bit Japanese.

I'm going to show Ruby. And tell her about my Heathcliff.

I went and called into The Blind Pig.

She wasn't in, though. Mr. Barraclough said, "Hello, young man." I wasn't even wearing my costume. Just being me.

He told me that Ruby had gone to dog obedience classes with Matilda. I walked up the back way, in case she was coming home, but I couldn't see her. And after five minutes, I gave up.

The moors were brooding in the dusk. A few sheep were baaing, but mostly there was just a swishing sound as a little breeze played on the grasslands. I would have to tell Honey and Flossie about the little breeze business.

I looked out over the land. It had seemed so bleak when I first came here, and now it seemed . . . well, so bleak. But I liked it more now.

I was so sad for Vaisey. It was horrible seeing her so upset. And she hadn't even been kissed yet.

At least I had. Well, if you could count the "bat trapped in the mouth."

Jo told me today that Phil said Ben thought I was too "immature" to go out with.

I would be upset, but then I had an image of him puffing along with a rucksack full of bricks.

I wish that I had Georgia around to give me some advice. I know she said, "A boy in the hand is worth two on the bus."

But what does that mean?

I had met Ben on a bus (nearly), so maybe that is what she meant. I had to wait for a boy who wasn't on a bus.

If I was going to come back to Dother Hall next term, I would get her to write down stuff for me. Like a guide to boys.

But I won't be coming back. I've only got 45 percent, which is a fail.

I can't even think about it. I find it hard to talk about things that mean a lot to me.

I wonder if the girls will miss me. I will miss them and I won't forget them.

And also, I have had a nearly boy friendy. Charlie did come and see the owlets with me, didn't he?

But I can't figure out what he meant by saying that thing about the cinema. That it would have been stupid if he had come.

Does he mean because I am too immature?

How am I supposed to get mature, unless someone gives me a hand becoming more maturerer? Jiminy cricket and also gadzooks.

I went off down the path home, and as I came round the corner of the lane by the pub, Cain was turning up the pathway toward me. Just as I stepped into a rabbit hole and fell over.

He looked down at me. Then he laughed.

He said, "This is fun, in't it?"

I said, "No, it's not."

He laughed meanly. "You love it, you follow me abaht. I see a lot of you, if you know what I mean."

I was thinking of something clever to say as I got up when I heard Alex's voice.

"All right, Cain?"

Mr. Darcy was here. He would see Heathcliff off.

Cain was still looking at me and didn't bother to turn to Alex. He just said, "Aye, not so bad."

Alex said, "Are you on your way home, Tallulah? I'll walk with you."

Cain said softly, "Mixing with the big boys now. Watch tha sen, Tallulah."

I didn't bother to reply to him, I just smiled at Mr. Darcy.

As I walked by, Cain slowly rubbed his chest with his hands. Oh my God, he was doing corker rubbing.

I said, "You really are . . ." And I couldn't think of a word bad enough.

Cain said, "Gorgeous? You love it." And he went off, whistling up the hill into the dark moorlands.

Alex said, "What was all that about?"

I said, "I don't know, he just picks on me. He's an awful person."

"Yeah, they're complicated lads, those Hinchcliffs."

"He's got a dog called Dog. And he just comes and looms over me. Looming."

"He probably likes you."

What?

Alex said, "Boys are a lot more nervous than you think."

Was he saying Cain was nervous?

I said, "He stubbed a cigarette out on the 'Absolutely No Smoking' sign. And he killed a fox. And was twirling it about."

Alex was walking along, letting me get it out of my system.

I said, "And, he told Jack to come, and Vaisey really likes him and they were getting on, and then Cain just says 'come,' and Jack goes like a little doggie. And now Vaisey is on the roof. It used to be Bob who was Mrs. Rochester, and now there are two of them."

Alex paused, but let the Mrs. Rochester thing go, and said, "A lot of boys are very status conscious. And Cain has a lot of status, so Jack will want to be like him."

I said, "Holy Mother of God, imagine WANTING to be like Cain."

Alex said, "Do you fancy visiting the owlets? I was going out but it got canceled."

Wow.

Mr. Darcy and me. Alone, looking at owlets.

I nodded, and tried a half smile and hair shake.

It felt good.

★ ★ ★

We walked down to the barn, and then Alex told me that he'd been seeing a girl but that they had split up. I didn't say "Good," even though it made me feel really funny. I tried an understanding smile, but I didn't know if he could see it, sideways on.

Anyway, I'm sure he was only telling me stuff because it was like he was telling Ruby. He, along with everyone else on the planet, probably thinks I am "immature."

Alex said, "Let's check that Connie's not around."

He opened the barn door and it was all quiet. He shone his torch into the corner where the nest was, and suddenly there was Connie.

Oh Jesus, Mary, and Joseph!!! Connie must have been sitting on Tallulah and Ruby, having a snooze. All right, my mother had a lot of faults but she doesn't sit on me when I'm in bed.

Connie started screeching and flapping her enormous wings out. Alex was backing out of the barn. He whispered, "We'd better get out of here."

We walked quickly down the pathway and I kept looking back, expecting to see a big shadow bearing down on us. It was so spooky. My heart was thumping.

Alex whispered, "Are you afraid of the dark?"

And as I said, "No," he lifted up his arms and went, "WaaaaaaAAAAA!"

And I leapt onto his back. Once my heart had stopped racing, it was quite funny. I laughed and laughed. It was probably relief from not being pecked to death by owls.

He gave me a piggyback for a bit, and then I got down.

I looked up at him and he looked back at me. And just for a tiny heart-stopping moment, I thought he was about to kiss me.

But he ruffled my hair and said, "Let's get you home, green-eyes."

Doesn't anyone besides Matilda want to kiss me?

When I woke up on Saturday morning, I wrote in my performance-art notebook a dream I had about Alex:

Alex came striding up to the Dobbinses' house, dressed in a white shirt and riding boots (and trousers).

He said he was going to take me out for a picnic on the moors.

I noticed my knees were at a normal height.

Lullah and Ruby the owlets came with us.

When we had our picnic, the owls had mouse sandwiches. We had pies.

Afterward, the owlets had a little sleep and I was running across the moors, laughing with Alex.

I put my foot down a rabbit hole and tripped over.

Alex picked me up and said, "You are so mature."

I looked up at him and raised my bottom eyelids.

And he changed into Charlie.

And then, as I slowly blinked, he turned into Cain.

He was singing, "She's Got the Corker-Rubbing Blues."

When I went down to breakfast, Dibdobs was sitting at the kitchen table with the lunatic brothers. She said, "Say good morning to Tallulah, boys!"

Sam and Max looked at me, and they both smiled at the same time.

They've got part of a proper tooth each!

I said, "You've got teeth, boys!!!"

Max said, "Did you hear me cleanin' my teef?"

Dibdobs was smiling proudly like she had grown the "teef" herself.

It was time to grow into my knees

I RUSHED OFF TO Dother Hall early because I was worried about Vaisey, and I thought I should tell her what Alex had said about the status boy stuff. I went up to the dorm and all the others were in there, talking on their beds. But there was no sign of Vaisey.

I said, "She's not still on the roof, is she?"

Ten minutes later, Vaisey came down. She is very pale but not crying.

I said, "Oh, my little friend, look at your sad hair."

I gave her a cuddle, but it made the tears come out of her again, so I thought I would do that thing that adults do to crying children. I went and got a big handkerchief from Milly, and then I got hold of Vaisey's nose with it and said, "Blow!"

It worked a little bit because she half smiled and said, "I've got a song to sing at the performance lunchtime."

She didn't come to any of the classes in the morning. Sidone has given her special permission to practice her song. If this is the state that you get in when you get a note from a boy, what is it like to have a real boyfriend?

We went into the theater for the lunchtime stuff.

Lavinia did a piece of avant-garde dance. With a beach ball. And Sidone complimented her on her "jazz hands."

I don't know what it was about, we were all so tense. And waiting to see whether Vaisey would sing or not. There was a long pause.

But then Sidone, in a chiffon hat, came back onstage and said, "Today, you are going to see live theater. Someone who is paying their dues. She didn't want to perform today because she has been very upset. But I told her, this is it, this is what Dother Hall is about. Show us your bleeding feet. Your bleeding heart."

And she went off, beckoning Vaisey out from the wings.

It was hard watching her walk on. Her hair looked so sad. Everyone was very quiet and still. And she was so pale. Where was the jolly red person?

Vaisey said to us, "I am going to sing a soul-music classic. I suppose some things are said so well that they can't be said any better."

And she stepped forward, into a single hard spotlight.

There was no accompaniment.

And she started to sing so beautifully:

You looked at me
It shook me
You tore me apart.
You've broken my
Tender, tender heart.

I woke up
We'd broke up
Before we could start.
I'll never forget you
Because I am so . . .
Bluuuuuueeeee
(Ooh-oooh-oooh)

Blimey, we were all wailing by the time she'd finished.

We gave her a big hug at the end and Blaise Fox said, "That's it, that's your big song for Cathy in *Wuthering Heights*. Marvelous, you'll have them weeping in the aisles! Keep the crying up, you'll look like a wreck."

We've been rehearsing *Wuthering Heights* for most of the day.

I think I am really getting into character.

I made Flossie laugh with my Yorkshire accent.

Even Vaisey giggled when I did my big "song" for her, which was mostly growling and kicking things.

As I was walking home, practicing my bad temper and surliness, and also trying to walk like Cain, Phil popped out from behind a tree and went, "Pssssst."

He said, "Tell the Tree Sisters to come to a late-night bonanza at the tree tonight, before we all go home."

I said, "What do you mean?"

He said, "I'll tell you what I mean: tell Jo, Flossie, Honey, and Vaisey, and, of course, your good self, to come to the tree at eight o'clock. We will bring stuff."

So I went all the way back to Dother Hall and told them.

Vaisey said she didn't want to go. But we persuaded her that it was probably one of the last times we would see the lads. In the end, she said she would. She is very brave, I think. Especially as Jack is going to be there. I wanted to say good-bye to Phil, and maybe Charlie would be there. My sort-of friend.

That night, at about half past seven, I set off up the path to Dother Hall for the final farewell tree fest. I waited by the back entrance whilst the girls crept out. They all had makeup on and had done their hair. I said to Vaisey, "You look lovely."

And she did. She looked pale but determined.

I had gone wild and put my Barely Pink lipstick on

and some mascara, and also I had borrowed a dress from Vaisey. It was time to grow into my knees.

We went off to our tree. And the boys were there already lying around under it.

Phil got hold of Jo and lifted her up. He said, "Whey hey hey!!"

Jo has told me that they are going to write to each other. She biffed him on his arms, which is her way of being affectionate, and he kissed her on the mouth. That left the rest of us feeling a bit awkward for a minute. Especially Jack, who looked like he was going to bite his lips off. Charlie wasn't there, but Ben was.

Oh dear.

Ben flopped over to me and held out his hand.

Again.

I said, "Hello, Ben."

And then he spotted Honey. She smiled and said, "That'th a nithe name, Ben." And he fell into her honey trap like a hypnotized bee. They were talking and laughing, and he played with her hair.

Oh, well. I sat down with Flossie and we opened some of the crisps that the boys had brought. They had a guitar as well and Jack started playing a little tune on it. He looked up at Vaisey and said to her, "Vaisey, will you come and sit and sing with me?"

And Vaisey said, "I'm not feeling very well."

Jack said, "Is that . . . because . . . Please come and talk to me, Vaisey."

Flossie and I didn't know what to do, so we just started talking loudly together.

Flossie said, "I quite like that Seth boy."

What???

I said, "He's a Hinchcliff, they are like wild animals."

Flossie started singing in a Southern accent. "Wild Seth, you make my heart sing . . . you make everything . . . Sethy!!!"

Then Charlie arrived.

I tried to pretend that I hadn't seen him.

He said, "Helllooooo, Tree Sisters! It's me!"

It was really good fun being in the woods at night with people singing and laughing and talking. Jack and Vaisey were half singing and half talking. I looked across at her and she smiled back at me.

Hoooray!!! Lawks-a-mercy and splice the mainbrace!!!

After about half an hour, Jo and Phil went off into the woods together.

Charlie was being very funny about Woolfe Academy—he's back there for another term. He said, "The headmaster says that he thinks a bit of responsibility will be the making of me. So he has made me team leader in the army corp."

And he winked at me and said, "Happy days."

Phil and Jo came dashing back.

Jo said, "Sidone and Monty are headed this way!!"

We said good night quietly and everyone hugged. Then the dorm girls headed back to Dother Hall and the boys went off to Woolfe. I looked after Charlie; this was probably the last time I would ever see him. As he disappeared into the trees, he did this really nice thing.

He blew a kiss to me.

How lovely was that?

I crept around the trees to get back to the road. I could see Monty and Sidone.

Sidone was doing a little dance with her scarf and I could hear Monty saying, "Marvelous, marvelous."

It was a soft night and I could hear owls hooting. I wonder if it is Connie out there with her friends. I would even miss Connie. And I couldn't bear to think of not seeing Lullah and Ruby. I must get big Ruby to send me notes and photos of them when I've left here.

As I was walking along, I heard something in the trees.

I hope it wasn't a bat.

A vampire bat.

Charlie stepped out. And said, "Yoo-hoo."

I looked at him and smiled.

He smiled back.

"I thought I would walk you back to Heckmondwhite."

I said, "What, in case I need to walk up some stairs and fall over?"

He said to me, "Lullah, that is a very random thing to say."

And I remembered that he had not been on the "date."

Which also reminded me that he had said it would have been "stupid" if he had been.

And that's when I thought I would show him the northern grit I'd learned whilst I've been here. My inner Emily Brontë.

I said, "Charlie, why did you say it would have been 'stupid' to have come to the cinema if I had been going?"

He came and stood near me and looked into my eyes.

I said, "I might be young and immature, but I am quite, you know . . ."

He said, "Tall?"

I said, "Well, yes, but I'm, well, there is no need for you to be ashamed to be seen with me."

Charlie looked at me. "Is that what you thought I meant? That I would have been embarrassed about you?"

I nodded.

He stroked my hair.

"Oh, Lullah. I am so sorry you thought that. I hate to think of you being upset. Look at your eyes in this light, they're like cats' eyes."

Was that a good thing?

And then he kissed me.

Softly on the mouth.

It felt really nice.

Then he did it again.

He had a lovely soft mouth.

It wasn't like the bat thing at all.

It was soft and melty.

Then he did it again, and put his arms around my waist and pulled me to him.

Oh, please, Gabriel, don't let me faint or fall down a rabbit hole or bang my head on a branch or . . .

Then he stopped.

He said, "Tallulah, I can't do this."

Oh no.

I said, "I could get better at kissing, if someone would help me. . . . It's just that I haven't—"

He hugged me to him.

"Lullah, it's nothing to do with that, it's nothing to do with you. You mustn't think that. And it's not that I don't want to. I do. But . . ."

But what?

He said, "I've got a girlfriend."

When I woke up, it was still dark. In my squirrel bed, I dreamt that I was up on the moors with the Brontë sisters. We were having a book club meeting and I said to Emily, "I've rewritten *Wuthering Heights* and now it has a happy ending. Heathcliff goes to dog obedience lessons with Matilda and the whole thing ends spiffingly." Then Heathcliff came striding toward us in his white shirt and breeches, and as he gets nearer I realize it is Charlie.

Charlie just looks at us and pours candle wax over his hands.

How could things go so nearly right all the time? First I'm kissed by Charlie, and then he tells me he has a girlfriend.

I suppose if it had been Cain he wouldn't have bothered to tell me.

It was a good job I was going home.

But I didn't want to go home.

Even one of the squirrel slippers has lost its tail. I could get Harold to sew it back on if I was staying here.

I got up and went to look out of the window. There was a low full moon, casting silver shadows amongst the trees and across the fields and moors.

It is the big performance of *Wuthering Heights* tomorrow. The headmaster from Woolfe Academy is coming and some of Monty and Sidone's "theater dahling" friends.

I was so restless and upset. In the end I gave up trying to go back to sleep. I thought I would go and see little Lullah and little Ruby. Everyone was in bed, so I went downstairs and opened the back door quietly. And as I did, I saw Connie swooping off, so the coast was clear. I walked down the path to the barn.

When I opened the barn door, there was someone in there holding one of the owlets. It was Lullah because I could see her legs sticking out.

I said, "Um, hello?"

And the figure turned round.

Cain.

Fondling the owls.

He'd better not be hurting them.

He said, "Oh, it's you. You get around for a lanky girl wi' nowt to her. Are you off back to your soft southern gaff?"

I said, "You are a complete bounder!"

He half smiled at me.

"Bounder? Is tha doing a bloody panto at that Dither Hall?"

I was so angry with him. Especially as I was practicing being him.

"You know what I mean, all that rock-star stuff, and Jack. And all those poor girls . . . You pick them up and put them down like they were toy girls. And then they leap into the river. And you just don't care, because you're so selfish."

He looked at me, with his dark eyes gleaming.

"Why ist tha blaming me? I can't help it, tha knows."

"What do you mean, you can't help it?"

He went and sat down, moodily poking the owlets with a little stick.

I said, "Don't do that, poking them."

He said, "They like it."

"They don't. Anyway, what do you mean, you can't help it?"

"I'm just a boy."

"That's ridiculous, I might as well say I'm just a girl."

"Tha can say that. Tha is a girl. . . ."

"I *know* that I'm a girl, thank you."

"Aye, let's not get carried away . . . tha's nearly a girl."

Suddenly I felt like I had grown into my knees. I said straight to his face, his black, hateful face, "Do you know what, Cain Hinchcliff, I hate you. It's quite a pleasant feeling."

He looked at me and said, "No, you dunt really. Tha just don't know what to mek of me. I make you feel funny."

I turned and stormed out of the barn.

Wearing the golden slippers of applause

WE ARE ALL IN the dressing room, getting ready for the show. Oh, I was so nervous. I hope I didn't have to go to the loo again, it took ages to get out of my breeches.

Ms. Fox gave us her pep talk before we took to the stage. It was: "Right, girls, this is it. Now then, remember what counts is this—it's not the preparation, it's not the costumes, it's not even how tall you are. . . . The main thing is . . . go out there and . . . BE GOOD!"

And that was it. Be good.

I've peeked through the curtains—the whole of Dother Hall is here to watch and some friends of Sidone's. And the headmaster of Woolfe Academy. I said to Jo, "That bloke with one leg must be the headmaster; Charlie told me about him."

Jo had a look. "Phil has given me a special friendship band to wear. We're going to write, and I hope that I'll see him, if, you know, I come back."

I said to her, "Of course you'll come back."

And I am sure she will. I am pretty sure all of them will. Even though they all do look very odd indeed.

Jo has devised her own costume for being thunder. It is some black trousers that are tight from the ankles to the knees and then really baggy round the bottom area, like she has pooed herself. She has big black headphones on and a dustbin lid attached to her chest which she is going to bang.

And she is loving every moment of it.

She gave me a big hug and said, "This is going to be great. You are going to be great."

Flossie and Honey are tuning up for the wind-singing. Honey is covered in veils and Flossie has a yashmak and harem pants on.

We've also made the set, which is Grimbottom with blasted oaks and painted waterfalls, and boulders made out of chicken wire and papier-mâché. It looks very atmospheric.

Monty came backstage to wish us luck. Monty has his mates Biffo and Sprogsy with him, and I think they might have had a sherry because Monty is wearing a kilt and sporran. He says it is the de Courcy clan tartan and then giggled a lot.

Just about ready to go on. Bob is cranking up the opening music. I am wearing breeches, a white shirt, and riding boots. I have got my hair scraped back into a ponytail and my eyebrows have got some eyebrow pencil on them.

Flossie said, "You don't need much."

She's right, my eyebrows are dark enough. In fact, with my hair back, I do look like Cain. Especially if I scowl.

Vaisey is wearing a dark wig and pale makeup. It's so odd not seeing her red hair bouncing around and glossy like she'd eaten a tin of dog food. She is "getting into character."

I don't need to get into character, I feel so mixed up and cross anyway. Seeing Cain really upset me. And I have just banged my head on the prop-cupboard door. I was looking for some more fake grass for one of the villagers to throw about.

The curtains went up and I took a big breath.

The performance started with Cathy and Heathcliff as children, playing on the moors.

I walked out first onto the stage and strutted about, kicking stuff and finding my inner wildness. Then I yelled, "Dog, dog, where the bloody hell art thee?"

And Matilda came on!!

She was my special surprise idea. I had worked out with Ruby that if I carried her squeaky bone, she would follow me around. Also, every time I say "Hooray" she lies on her back and puts her legs in the air because of her dog obedience classes. If I want her to go off, I just chuck her squeaky bone into the wings and she scampers off after it. Milly and Tilly feed her doggie treats until it is time for her to come on again.

I think she should definitely audition for the West End stage.

In the first bit, Cathy and I are all happy together, apart from when we fight and squabble. And even though the weather is often very bad (Jo, Flossie, and Honey flitting and banging and singing and crashing into one another) Cathy and I enjoy just being together. And making our own fun. Because we are in love. And it makes us dance with joy.

At the bit when I was teaching Cathy my Irish dancing there was spontaneous applause from the audience. And for the very first time I felt the slippers of applause!

The second half was much darker. Heathcliff hears Cathy saying to a village person (Becka), "I would no more marry Heathcliff than die, he's rough and coarse and dark."

And Heathcliff goes off to London, brokenhearted.

Then Cathy is heartbroken because he is gone.

Vaisey sings her big song:

> *I woke up*
> *We'd broke up*
> *Before we could start.*

I'll never forget you
Because I am so . . .
Bluuuuuueeeee
(Ooh-oooh-oooh)

It was amazing, we all watched from the wings.

Monty and his mates had their handkerchiefs out and were weeping.

THEN I come back from London. Much, much more cross than when I went. I've got a jacket and a scar and my mustache. And sideburns.

The wind gathers and Cathy shivers as she sees me. I stopped in the middle of the stage. Just looking at the audience. Moodily, I paced up and down. I kicked a boulder. I didn't flinch. Then I shouted, "DOG!" And squeaked my squeaky bone.

And Matilda came on.

In a leather jacket. And shades.

It brought the house down!!

At the end, when Cathy died and was scrabbling at my window (Tilly on a box with a window frame) I started a band and "sang" a song about her: "I know you are dead, but it doesn't have to be the end. . . ."

I growled it out and strutted around, like a rock star. And for the final chorus, did Irish dancing by myself, in a mean and moody way.

I was improvising and jumping high and throwing my

legs around. It made everyone really laugh. And applaud.

Backstage, Ms. Fox gave me a slap on the back and said, "Quite amazing. The squeaky bone was a stroke of comedy genius. And your legs . . ."

We were all high as kites afterward. And when we went back to take another bow, Sidone came onto the stage and said to the audience, "Once again, we see the magic of theater. Who would have thought we would see these little embryos fill the stage? Absolutely FILL the stage. Congratulations, congratulations, and we will see you all next term."

At first I thought that I had heard wrong. But it's true. I can come back next term!! The Dream is not over!! I am coming back to Dother Hall.

Hoorayyyy!!

Gadzooks.

Spiffing.

Back in my squirrel room, I'm saying good-bye to Heckmondwhite. I will miss my little squirrel room. In fact, I think I will ask Dibdobs if I can take my squirrel slippers home to keep me company until I come back.

I went down into the kitchen and Dibdobs was sitting at the kitchen table with the lunatic brothers. She said, "Hellooooooo, Tallulah. Say hellllllooooo to Tallulah, boys."

Sam said, "Oo going seepin?"

Aaaah.

Dibdobs said, "Come and join us, we've got toothpicks and we are making alien vegetables, aren't we, boys?"

Sam said, "Valien bum bums."

Dibdobs said, "That's a silly word, isn't it, bum bums?"

Max smashed his courgette down, "S'nice!"

Sam said, "You're a BUM BUM!!!"

And they both started laughing madly and jabbing at each other with courgettes.

Dibdobs was trying to be calm. "Don't jab each other with the courgettes, boys."

I went for a last look around Heckmondwhite. Across the village green, I saw the bus from Skipley screech to a halt at the bus stop. Mr. Barraclough got off.

I tucked myself back in the shadows. I don't think I could take any more horsie jokes.

Mr. Barraclough shouted back into the bus, "If there is any lasting damage from that bloody duck attacking my nether regions, I will be in touch, Job Earnshaw, so be said. My nether regions are my livelihood."

And he went limping up to The Blind Pig.

I'm going to miss all this.

But not for long.

Because I have filled my Withering Tights . . . and I

will return to fill them again.

I've written a letter to Ruby and I'm going to give it to her to read after I've caught my train today.

> Dear Rubster,
> Ay up!! Just to say, look after little Lullah and little Ruby till we all get back. Tell them that we'll take them on a mouse picnic in September, if there is no fog.
> I'll really miss you but it's not long till next term. I'll bring you your own lipstick and Matilda a special bonio. Oh, and I forgot to tell you about Charlie and me, but I'll tell you when I see you.
> Watch that Cain.
> See you soon, fun-sized friend.
> Love,
> Loobylullah xxx
>
> P.S. My corkers are definitely on the move. Toodle pip for now.

Tallulah's glossary

apple catchers

These are attractive huge pants. Pants that are big enough to collect a lot of apples in.

Another term for this sort of commodious pant is "harvest festivals" (i.e., all is safely gathered in).

bagsie

If you say this it means, "Oy, that is mine," meaning "Oy, I have bagged that." It's probably an old poacher's term. And believe me, there are a lot of old poachers in the North.

barm pot

A fruitcake. If you say, "You barm pot" it's not like saying, "You loonie"; it's more sort of affectionate.

Like saying: "Oooh, you slight idiot."

bejesus

This is from Hiddly Diddly land (Oireland). It's a not-too-naughty swear. Like "Oh my word, you caught me on the knee with that hockey ball."

Or, gadzooks.

Is that any help?

No, I thought not.

Boots

A large drugstore chain selling mostly cosmetics.

The Brontë sisters

Em, Chazza, and Anne. They lived in Haworth in Yorkshire in . . . er . . . well, a while ago. And they wrote *Wuthering Heights*, *Jane Eyre*, and loads of other stuff about terrible weather conditions and moaning. But in a good way.

cat's pajamas

When someone (like Cain for instance) thinks they are just too great for words. Like when a cat is so full of itself it shows off in its pajamas.

OK, I've never really seen cats out shopping for pajamas, but they must do it sometime. Otherwise why would this be a saying?

Grammar never lies.

corkers

Another word for girls' jiggly bits.

Also known as norkers.

Honkers, etc.

Cousin Georgia calls them "nunga-nungas."

She says because when you pull them out like an elastic

band, they go nunga-nunga-nunga.

I will be the last to know whether this is true or not.

corker harness

Something to hold the corkers pert and not too jiggly.

A bra.

The Dane

Hamlet.

All actors do this. Refuse to tell you what's going on.

It's like never saying "*Macbeth*," and always calling it "the Scottish play."

If we all did this, where would we be?

I don't know.

No one would know.

Mr. Darcy (and Mrs. Rochester)

Two characters well known for their sense of fun. Not.

Mr. Darcy was in *Pride and Prejudice* and at first he was all snooty and huffy; then he fell in a lake and came out with his shirt all wet. And then we all loved him. In a swoony way.

Mrs. Rochester was Mr. Rochester's secret wife in *Jane Eyre* that he kept in a cupboard upstairs. She was mad as a snake and would only wear her nightie.

In the end it all finished happily because she set fire to the house, went up on the roof for a bit of a dance about, and tripped over her nightie and fell to her death.

Leaving Mr. Rochester blind.

This is one of Em, Chazza, and Anne's more comic novels.

dunderwhelp

A polite Yorkshire way of saying: "You are an absolute disgrace of a person. Look at your knees."

egg cozies

Little knitted hats for keeping boiled eggs warm.

fogwear

Yes. What is fogwear?

A car headlight strapped to your cap perhaps?

A foghorn handbag?

It doesn't matter. No one is going to see it anyway.

garyboy

Anyone called Gary is a gay person. By that I mean Cain, Seth, and Ruben Hinchcliff say this. And even if someone called Gary wasn't gay at first, he would be by the time he had been told he was for fourteen years.

get a cob on

To have the monk on.

You don't know what that means either, do you?

Erm . . .

To have a face like a smacked arse.

Does that help?

Well, I'm trying to help, don't get a cob on.

ginnel

Now this is Viking. It is. I do know this.

A ginnel is a narrow passageway that runs between two sets of terraced houses. So there is a wall on either side. And it's narrow.

I don't know why the Vikings had anything to do with it, though, because terraced houses weren't invented when they were in Yorkshire pillaging stuff.

gogglers

Eyes.

To goggle is to look at stuff.

If you couldn't see anything then you would need gogs.

golden slippers of applause

Sidone, the revered and possibly mentally unstable principal of Dother Hall, has her own unique view of the world.

Especially the showbiz world.

In this world she is obsessed by feet.

So her opposite of the "golden slippers of applause" is "the bleeding feet of rejection."

Heathcliff

The "hero" of *Wuthering Heights*. Although no one knows why.

He's mean, moody, and possibly a bit on the pongy side.

Cathy loves him, though. She shows this by viciously rejecting him and marrying someone else for a laugh. Still, that is true love on the moors for you.

heavens to Betsy

An expression of astonishment like . . .

"Gosh!"

Or, "Crikey!"

Or, as they say in Yorkshire:

"Well, I'll go to the top of our stairs!"

I know it makes little sense but believe me it's best not to argue about these things with Yorkshire folk. Or they will very likely get a cob on.

(see previous)

hiddly diddly diddly

The sound of all Irish songs (and dances). It fits them all.
Try it.

Iron Man group

An all-men's group that hangs around with other men so that they can find their inner man-iness.

Usually they knit a lot.

In caves.

jazz hands

Sidone loves jazz hands.

Essentially it's sticking your hands out a lot while lurching around to jazz.

lawks-a-mercy

"Crikey" but longer.

loosey-goosey

You know. All floppy. Like a floppy—er—goose.

manky pillock

"Manky" means "smelly," and "pillock" . . . well, "pillock" is a combination of "dunderwhelp" and "barm pot" with just a hint of the "garyboy."

mardy bum

Someone who is so bad-tempered and "mardy" that even their bottom is annoyed.

Like Beverley when she found out that although she was engaged to Cain (she bought her own ring), he had two other girlfriends.

Which is why she flung herself in the river.

And ruined her dress because the river was only two inches deep.

Mummers play

Not a mummy's play, which is what I thought at first. Because a mummy's play would be quite dull. People all wrapped up in bandages and dead.

No, a Mummers play was in medieval times, when actors

would dress up in rags with their faces painted blue and go into pubs to entertain people.

They would do this by pretending to fight and hit the audience over the head with sheep's bladders.

Much like The Blind Pig at the weekend.

nobbliness

I'm on firmer ground here.

Nobbly bits are usually bony bits that look, well, nobbly.

I have loads of it.

In the knee area.

noddy niddy noddy

A person who doesn't have much furniture upstairs.

Or to make it clearer: A person who has the lights on, but no one is home.

northern grit

Umph and determination. If you say to a northern person:

"Don't go out in that storm, you barm pot. The rain is coming down so hard you will be reduced to half your height."

The Northerner would say:

"What rain?"

And go out in his underpants.

"On Ilkley Moor Bar T'at"

A song about someone who goes out on Ilkley moor without a hat.

Yes it is.

There is probably another one that goes, "Went down t'shops to get some lard."

quakebottom

Someone who is so nervous and frightened that even their bottom is shaking.

rufty tufty

tough (tuf)

and

rough (ruf)

and ty (ty)

shuffle-ball change

A tap-dancing technique, i.e., hopping.

sjuuuge

When toddlers don't have many teeth (or brains) they can't say words properly. So this means "huge."

Either that or they do know how to say "huge" and are just being annoying.

Maybe toddlers can really secretly talk from birth.

I bet they can read as well.

They are just having a laugh.

And being lazy.

Sled-werk

An artistic term used to describe the "Sled-ists" of Norway, who painted with sledges.

So Georgia tells me.

splice the mainbrace

A bit like "Swab the poop deck!"

A nautical term of astonishment.

Like "Shiver my timbers" and "Left hand down a bit."

yarooo!

"Hurrah" only spelled wrong.

Yeppity doo dah

I think this can be laid firmly at the feet of the American nation.

It was the Americans who invented a song called "Zip-A-Dee-Doo-Dah," and because that made little sense we now say "Yeppity doo dah."

To mean "yes."

THE SHOW MUST GO ON!
HERE'S A SNEAK PEEK AT
TALLULAH'S NEXT
(MIS)ADVENTURE:

A MiDSUMMER TiGHTS DREAM

Back on the showbiz express

PERFORMING ARTS COLLEGE, HERE I come again! Hold on to your tights!! Because I am holding on to mine, I can tell you. Which makes it difficult to go to the loo, but that is the price of fame. And fame is my game!

Once more I am chugging back to Dother Hall. Or "the theater of dreams" as Sidone Beaver, the principal, calls it. I am truly on the showbiz express of life.

Well, the stopping train to Skipley, the Entertainment Capital of the North. Or home of the West Riding Otter, as some not-showbiz people call it. I don't think they mean that only a big fat otter lives in the town, although you never know!

Hooray and chug-a-lug-a-doo-dah.

I feel like shouting out to the heavens. I think I will.

I can now because the grumpy woman with the stick got off at the last stop. Oh, the Northern folk with their jolly Northern ways. She was so grumpy about her gammy leg. She said the stick had worn down on one side so that she fell over in strong winds. I didn't ask her any of this—she just told me. But hey-nonny-no, as Shakespeare said. I am going to pull down the window and shout out loud:

"The name is Tallulah. Tallulah Casey!!! And I'm back. I'm moving up! Moving on up! Nothing can stop me! Yes, I used to be shy and gangly with nobbly knees and no sticky-out bits. No corkers. I was corkerless. I didn't even wear a corker holder. But now even my corkers are on the move!"

Especially when the train keeps stopping unexpectedly. What now? Maybe the West Riding Otter is on the line. The tannoy is crackling but I can only hear heavy breathing and snuffling. Lawks a mercy, the wild otter has hijacked the train!

He wants to make people understand that otters have feelings too. They're not just furry fools—

Ooomph.

Oooooh blimey, I nearly shot into the opposite seat then because we're lurching off again.

Woo-hoo!

Anyway, I'm being giddy about the otter. He can't really be driving the train because he couldn't reach the driving wheel. Unless he's got stilts. And it doesn't say

Skipley is the home of the West Riding Circus Otter. With his big shoes.

I don't care about the otter driver! Live and let live, I say.

Uh-oh, the tannoy is crackling again.

"Sorry about that, ladies and gentlemen, I momentarily lost hold of my pie. Next stop Skipley."

We're just passing Grimbottom Peak. Brr. It looks so dark and forbidding up there. I'm surprised it's not pouring down with rain and . . . It is pouring down with rain.

Crumbs, it's like the lights have been turned off. You can hardly see Grimbottom. The locals say that when day-trippers are up there the fog can come down in minutes. Mr. Bottomly at the post office once told me and Flossie:

"One minute t'day-trippers are up there on't top, playing piggy in't middle like barm pots. The next it's so dark they can't even see t'ball. And it's in their hand. Hours later the grown-ups stumble home but the little'uns are nivver seen no more. Sometimes late at night tha can hear 'em up there wailing, 'Mummeee . . . Dadeeeee . . .' All them lost bairns, speaking from beyond the grave."

Flossie said, "That's rubbish. There's a massive wild dog up there called Fang. Half dog, half donkey, and it comes out in the fog and takes the children and raises them as its puppies."

In my opinion, even though I haven't known her for

long, my new friend Flossie is what is commonly known as "mad."

But mad or not, I am really, really excited about seeing her and my new mates again. Vaisey and Flossie and little Jo and Honey, who can't say her "r"s, but knows everything about boys. She says she always has "two or thwee on the go."

We can go into the woods near Dother Hall again, to our special place! And gather round our special tree. Our special tree where we met the boys from Woolfe Academy when they surprised us doing our special dance that Honey taught us. She said we had to be proud of all of ourselves, even the bits we didn't like. It was a "showing our inner glory" dance. Or "inner glowee" as Honey called it. Which in my case was hurling my legs around shouting, "I love my knees, I love them!!!"

Not quite as embarrassing as Vaisey waggling her bottom at the tree, but close.

The Woolfe Academy boys, well, Charlie and Phil, call us the "Tree Sisters."

Charlie said to me . . .

Well, I won't think about Charlie. Not after what happened after he kissed me.

Where was I in my performing life? Oh yes, when I got to Dother Hall I couldn't do anything. The others could sing and dance and act, but all I could do was be tall and do a bit of Irish dancing.

I was convinced that I would never be asked back and that I would never wear the golden slippers of applause. Things changed when Blaise Fox, the dance tutor, saw my Sugar Plum Bikey performance. My ballet based on the Sugar Plum Fairy—only done on a bicycle. The one when my ballet skirt got caught in the back wheel, and I accidentally shot off my bike and destroyed the backstage area. I remember what she said.

She said: "Tallulah Casey, watching you is like watching someone whose pants are on fire." Then she asked me to play Heathcliff in *Wuthering Heights* at the end of last term. And the rest is showbiz legend.

Heathcliff's Irish-dancing solo was a triumph! And, also, not so easy in tight trousers.

I still don't know why she cast me as Heathcliff though.

Perhaps I really do look like a boy?

If I look down and squint my eyes a bit, I can definitely see pimply bumps in the corker area.

No one can argue with that. The front of a jumper never lies.

My jumper is one of the ones Cousin Georgia and her Ace Gang chose for me. It's green and she says it goes with my eyes and gives me je ne sais quoi.

Well, she actually said, "It says 'ummmmmmmm' but not 'oooohhhh, look at me, I'm a tart.'"

Nearly at Skipley. I'm so excited. This is going to be my Winter of Love, I can tell.

When I stayed with Cousin Georgia on my way back from summer school it was brilliant. I haven't really spent a lot of time with her before because of being in Ireland and having crap parents who actually do stuff. Not just bake tarts or DIY like everyone else's parents. Not good old boring stuff. My mum goes off and paints and my dad goes off exploring to find endangered things. He collects mollusks mostly but I think last time he found a rare hairy potato. He's like a cross between David Bellamy and . . . a Labrador. That is not a proper dad in anyone's language.

That's a Labradad.

Hee. I think that might very nearly be a joke.

I'm going to put it into my performance-art notebook that I will be keeping.

I've got a special new notebook with a black glossy cover and some plums on the front of it.

It's really arty, and er . . . fruity.

I've already made my first entry.

It says:

Winter of Love.

I'll just add my "Labradad" idea.

Labradad. A portrait of a dad who is half pipe-smoking bloke and half Labrador. He's confused between the two worlds. Between pipes and sticks. I'm thinking an improvised dance piece. Perhaps the Labradad fetching sticks. Or pipes?

Or ducks?

Hmmmmm.

I love my parents but they're not normal. Or around much. But they have let me come back to Dother Hall—even though I'm not allowed to board.

It was great staying with Cousin Georgia. It was brilliant on the boy front as well.

She got her Ace Gang round to teach me "wisdomosity" and also "snogging techniques." We all tucked up in her bed, which was cozy.

Georgia said, "Have a jammy dodger and give us the goss snogwise."

All the gang were wearing false beards to help me get into the mood.

So . . . I told her about going to the cinema in Skipley with some boys from Woolfe Academy. I told her about my first kiss. With floppy Ben. And how it was like having a little bat trapped in my mouth.

Her Ace Gang looked at me. Then Georgia said, "Are you a fool with just a hint of an idiot thrown in?"

Then they gave me their wisdomosity about boys. And snogging.

Gosh, Georgia knows a lot.

About varying pressure of the lips, what to do with

your tongue (don't waggle it about like a fool), the scoring system for snogging. (Number 1 to Number 10, I can't remember all of them but I do remember Number 4 is "a kiss lasting over three minutes without a break." You need a mate for that one, so that they can time it for you.)

Honestly. I couldn't believe it.

I'm dying to try out my new skills.

The amount she knew, she must have spent most of her time doing snogging research.

I said that to her and she said, "I did, my strange gangly cousy. But I have put aside snogging to teach you the ways of boydom. I do it because I luuurve you. But not in a lezzie way."

Which is good.

I think.

What is a "lezzie way"?

I think it's to do with girl snogging.

But I didn't ask.

Oh chuggy-chug-chug. Come on, train!!!

I wonder what time the rest of the Tree Sisters will arrive tomorrow?

Oh, here we are at the train station. Hurrah!!! There's its sign swinging in the biting gale force wind. Just as I remember:

Skipley Home of the West Riding Otter

Hang on a minute, some Northern vandal has painted a "b" and a "y" over the otter bit. So now it reads:

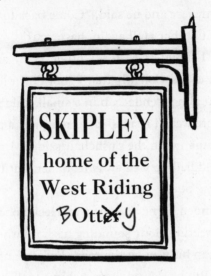

SKIPLEY
home of the
West Riding
BOtter̶y̶

I have just got off the showbiz express and now I am getting on the bus of hope. Which will transport me to . . . The Theater of Dreams.

I can see the bus driver through the closed door, sitting in the driver's seat. I recognize him from last term. I wonder if he recognizes me?

As I hauled my bag on board up the steps he put the pipe to one side of his mouth and shouted, "Stop messing about and get on if you're getting on, merry legs. It's bloody parky with that door open."

I said, "Why did you call me merry legs?"

He said, "Because you're lanky and your legs are all over the shop."

I paid my fare and he said, "Come back to prat around like a fool at Dither Hall again, have you?"

Before I could say "It's Dother Hall, actual—" he accelerated off so violently that I shot down to the end of the bus and almost ended up in a small child's pushchair. Luckily there wasn't a small child in it, just a pig.

The woman with the pushchair said, "Mind my pig."

I am huddled up well away from her, but I think I can still smell pig poo.

We bumped along the road to Heckmondwhite. The driver is careering along sounding his horn whenever there is anything in his way on the road. Pedestrians. Bicyclists. A cow pat. But he slowed down behind a lollipop lady who was walking home. With her sign. She tried to let him pass but he cheerily waved her on and drove slowly behind her. Then for no reason when we got to a sharp corner he revved up and blasted his horn and she fell into a hedge. He was laughing so much I thought he might swallow his pipe.

I couldn't help being excited. This is like a postcard of a winter scene in Yorkshire. There is even some snow on the top of Grimbottom Peak. And I shivered as I thought about Fang up there. Raising his fictitious children as fictitious puppies.

Winter of Love

WE ARRIVED AT THE bus stop in Heckmondwhite just as it was getting dark. In my Dother Hall brochure it says, "Heckmondwhite has its own 'zany' cosmopolitan atmosphere."

I don't know that most people would call a village green and a post office and a pub called The Blind Pig "zany." Unless you counted the knitted flags over the village hall.

I bet the Dobbinses, my substitute parents, have got something to do with that.

Maybe I should just nip quickly over to the pub and see my fun-sized friend, Ruby, and my four-legged mate Matilda, her bulldog? I could give her the lipstick I've bought her. Not Matilda, Ruby. Dogs don't wear makeup. But what they do wear is the little ballet tutu I have got for her from Pets Party shop. I hope it will go round her waist. She is quite porky in the middle.

And anyway, even if Rubes was out I could leave the presents with her older brother, Alex. Alex the dream boy. Alex with his long limbs and his longish thick chestnut hair. And his two eyes. And his back and front . . . and everything. And we could chat about performing arts. He's gone off to Liverpool to do rep there and I could chat about my performance plans. Maybe discuss my Labradad idea.

Maybe not. I don't want him to think of me as a bloke with a pipe fetching sticks.

Don't Miss Tallulah's Next Adventure!

Will Tallulah be able to test out her new snogging skills and ace her performance in this term's project, *A Midsummer Night's Dream*? Only time and more Irish comedy dancing will tell.

HARPER TEEN
An Imprint of HarperCollinsPublishers

www.epicreads.com